BECOMING K-9

A BOMB DOG'S MEMOIR (K-9 HEROES, BOOK 1)

RADA JONES

Illustrated by
MARIAN JOSTEN

APOLODOR

This book is a work of fiction. Names, characters, places, and incidents are the product of the author's imagination or are used fictitiously. Any resemblance to actual events, locales, or persons, living or dead, is entirely coincidental.

APOLODOR PUBLISHING

ABOUT THIS BOOK

Hello, reader. Guinness and I are glad you're here.

This K-9 memoir is a work of fiction. Dogs don't write much, and they publish even less. And while they can read into our souls, their spelling is nothing to write home about.

That's why I had to be the one to write Guinness's story. She's the fourth German shepard that I belonged to, and as they crossed the rainbow bridge, they each left a void in my soul that nothing can fill, not even the next dog. They took care of me for a while, then left me drifting dejected until the next one came along to guide me and love me, whether I deserved it or not, and make me a better human. Be glad you didn't meet me before.

Thank you all, Kirby, Xena, Gypsy, and Guinness, for your love, care, and supervision. No matter how hard I tried to learn from you, I still can't tell goose guano from duck poop. But I did learn to hear your thoughts.

So I wrote this, out of love to you, and all the dogs who make the world a better place.

Rada

ALSO BY RADA JONES

Dedication

To dogs:

May you spend forever with your loved ones. You deserve it.

To humans:

May you become the person your dog thinks you are.

Outside of a dog, a book is man's best friend. Inside of a dog it's too dark to read.

— Attributed to Groucho Marx

BECOMING K-9

1

Who knew training humans was so hard? You'd wonder why. They aren't that stupid. It takes them a while, but they eventually learn when you want out, you're hungry or you're thirsty. They can even talk to each other by making noise with their tongue. How weird is that? Even my brother Blue, who's the slowest of us all, knows that the tongue is for lapping water and panting to cool down.

Mom cocked her head and licked my nose.

"That's the best they can do, dear. They have no tails, their ears don't move, and most don't even have enough fur to raise their hackles. No wonder they're confused and need us to guide them. And that's what we do; that's our life's work. But we need to choose them carefully."

Mom was on her sixth litter and very wise. Beautiful, too, with her long muzzle, amber eyes, and smooth, shiny fur, all black but for her golden legs and loving pink tongue.

She glanced at Yellow, who chased his tail instead of paying attention, and growled. He hung his head and sat in line with the rest of us to listen.

It was a lovely summer day as Mom homeschooled us in Jones's front yard. The warm wind tickled my nose. I bit it, but I caught nothing. I tried again, but Mother threw me a side glance, so I closed my mouth and sat still.

"Boys and girls, today's the day. People will come to check you out and choose which one to take home. They don't know it, but it doesn't work that way. You choose your humans, but choose them wisely. Sniff them all, then pick the ones that smell like food if you want a good life. You may sometimes get bacon, maybe even grapes. Humans say dogs don't eat grapes, but that's poppycock. They just want to keep them for themselves. My grandma was a pure-bred Alsatian, and she loved Riesling. I never had Riesling, but Concord isn't bad."

A shiny strip of drool dripped from Mom's mouth. She licked it off and inspected us. We were seven: three boys and four girls. But that doesn't much matter when you're just ten weeks old. The only difference is how you pee. The boys don't know how to squat so they need something to lift their leg to, like a bush or a mailbox. How stupid!

"Why don't you just lift your leg, if that's what you need to do? What does the bush have to do with anything?"

Mom bristled.

"Leave them alone, Red."

I tried, but it was hard. I was the runt of the litter, so I had to prove myself all the time. Mom said I had a Napoleonic complex.

"What's that?"

"It's when you're the smallest, so you have to be meaner to show them that size doesn't matter."

I told you Mom is brilliant. She came all the way from Germany when she was just a pup. Our human, Jones, has two passions: German shepherds and history. Mom was his first German shepherd, and he spent lots of time teaching her things most dogs never heard about.

He still does, even now that she's old. He sits in his recliner and reads to her as she lays by the fireplace. Sometimes I listen in. There was a story about a dude named Hitler. Not a nice guy, but for loving German shepherds. Another one about that short guy Napoleon who tried to conquer the world while wearing funny hats. And one about some place called Afghanistan.

"That's a bad war, Maddie," Jones said, scratching the four white hairs in his beard. "Those Taliban, they are not nice people."

He calls her Maddie, but her real name is Madeline Rose Kahn Van Jones. He is Jones. The Van is for Van Gogh, some orange dude who got so mad he bit off his own ear. The rest is just for show, since people pay more for dogs with long names; they call that a pedigree. Mom's pedigree is longer than her tail.

As always, Mom was right. People came to see us, and they brought their spouses, their kids, and even their dogs to check us out and choose which one to get. Like, really? Jones said that only one out of twenty German shepherd owners is smarter than his dog. I don't believe it. I bet he fudged the numbers to feel better. You think you own a dog? Who feeds who? Who cleans after who? Who does the work, everything but making decisions? You, human, in case you didn't know it. You don't buy a dog; you hire supervision. But I digress.

My littermates and I wore colored collars so humans could tell us apart. There was no need, really, since we were all different, but humans couldn't see it. What color did I wear? Red, of course. I was small, but I was the queen of the litter, whether the others liked it or not.

A fat man in a Hawaiian shirt stopped to stare at me. He called his female.

"Look at this red one! Isn't he cute?"

She hobbled closer, leaning on her crooked stick. I love sticks, so I tried to take it. She didn't want to let go, but I insisted. They laughed.

"Let's get him."

Jones cleared his throat.

"Red is lovely, indeed, but she's a very active little person who needs a lot of attention. How much time do you plan to work with her every day?"

"Work with her?"

"Yes. Walk her, train her, and play with her."

They stared at him like he'd lost his marbles. He smiled.

"May I recommend Brown here? He's lovely, easygoing, and eager to please. He'll be happy to lay on the sofa watching TV. Or Miss Green? She's a polite little lady who gets along with everyone and never disappoints."

Brown left. So did Green, Yellow, and even White, while I stayed, waiting for my forever home.

"Take it easy, Red dear," Mother said when there were only two of us left—Black and me. "You need to soften up a bit; otherwise, you'll be left without a family. People look for easygoing dogs to fit into their lives, not for somebody to take charge. Though maybe they should, really, but they aren't smart enough to know that."

Her German accent made her words feel harsh. Have you ever listened to Germans? It's like they're constipated while they also have a cold. They keep clearing their throats, so their words come out like bullets from a machine gun. I don't speak German, but I love watching old war movies with Jones.

"What do you mean, Mom? What should I do?"

"Lick their hands, sweetheart. Wrap yourself around their feet and stare at them like they hung the moon."

"Are you serious?"

"Of course."

"But they're stupid!"

"Come on, Red, don't be so judgmental. You're just a pup, and you have so much to learn. A nice family will give you a good life. They'll love you, play with you, and spoil you. Knowing you have a good, safe home will lift a weight off my soul."

You think I listened? You've got to be kidding.

That's how I ended up in the military.

2

When the last family stopped by to pick up Black and I was left behind, Mom got upset. She licked me all over to give me a nice bath, but I knew she wasn't happy.

"That's OK, Mom. I'd rather stay here with you and Jones than go with those stupid humans. They don't even have tails. Even worse, they don't have the common sense of a cat."

Mom shook all over like she'd been out in the rain. She was dry, but that's how she disagreed. Why shake just your head when you can make a stronger statement?

"You can't stay here, Red. We aren't a breeding program; we're just a little family business. Jones can't afford to keep us both. I'm old, and I'm not worth much to anyone but him. I'm afraid you'll have to go."

"Go where?"

"Wherever he finds you a job. He loves you, and he'll do his best, but I'm afraid you won't get to be a spoiled pet living the good life with a nice family."

"I don't want to be a spoiled pet living with a nice family."

"What do you want, Red?"

"I want...I want to go for long walks and smell new things and eat bacon and be free."

Mom sighed.

"I'm sorry to break it to you, baby, but you're a dog. Dogs no longer run free. Our ancestors gave that up thousands of years ago when they decided to share people's fire and eat their food. These days, our life revolves around humans. I hope yours will be kind, loving, and smart enough to appreciate everything you have to offer."

"I'll bite them if they don't. I have sharp teeth."

Mom looked away, and for a moment, I thought she was hiding tears. But that can't be. Number one, dogs don't cry. And number two...I forgot what number two was. So I went to chew on Jones's boots for a while, trying to remember. Chewing always helps me focus. But I couldn't remember, not even after I finished the left heel. Even worse, they weren't real leather, so that night, I got sick all over the kitchen. Mom cleaned it up, and Jones never knew. Well, not until he wore the boots, that is.

I was thirteen weeks by then, and my brothers and sisters were all gone, so I got to chill with Mom and Jones. That was the life. We went for long walks every morning, then we napped and re-napped. In the evenings, we watched old movies and munched on crunchy buttered popcorn.

But then the days got shorter, and the sun lost its power. One day, as Mom and I played in the yard, waiting for Jones to drive us to the park, a burst of wind shook off a bunch of yellow leaves that fell on us like rain.

"The fall's here," Mom said.

"The fall of what?"

She cocked her head to think better.

"Good question, Red. The fall of leaves, I guess. It gets cold, so the leaves turn yellow and red, then fall off."

"What do the trees do?"

"They wait for spring to come back. That's how life goes."

Jones turned on the radio.

"To everything, there is a season; to everything, there is a reason."

Mom perked her ears, then lifted her muzzle to the sky and started howling with the music.

"There's a time to be born, and a time to die; a time to plant, and a time to reap; a time to kill, and a time to heal; a time to laugh, and a time to weep."

The song stirred something inside me. I lifted my nose to the sky and howled with Mom. I didn't understand the words, but the melody came from deep in my soul, and I couldn't stop singing like I couldn't stop breathing.

Jones's jaw dropped. He stared at us, then shook his head and laughed.

"I didn't know the Byrds sang the song of your people, but I'd be darned if it doesn't make sense."

That evening he looked up the song.

"I got something for you, girls."

When that haunting song filled the house, Mom and I sang along. Jones joined us.

"A time to kill, and a time to heal; a time to laugh, and a time to weep."

I didn't know it then, but my time to leave was coming.

3

A few days later, two men in a Jeep came by. The short one was old, the young one was tall, and they both wore khaki.

Jones took me out to meet them, and Mom followed.

"Thanks for coming, folks. This is Red. She's an opinionated young lady with a high prey drive, and she's fearless."

I glance at Mom.

"What's he saying?"

"That you're good at catching fast things, dear. It's a compliment."

It doesn't really feel that way, with him looking gloomy and all, but I don't have time to ponder. The young man slaps his hip in command and screeches:

"Hey, Pup. Come here."

I sit on my butt and ogle him down my nose.

"Like really? You think I'll have any random Tom, Dick, or Harry tell me what to do? Young whippersnapper, if you want us to get acquainted, you'll have to do the work."

The short one laughs. He's small and wiry, with warm eyes and a few white hairs floating above his pink head.

"She's got a personality, doesn't she? All thirty pounds of her, and she's tough as nails."

He offers me his hands to sniff.

He had Michigans for lunch. That's our North Country specialty—hot dogs with garlicky meat sauce and raw onions. They're delicious, but you want to spit out the onions, especially if you plan on a date. But he doesn't look like he's into dating. He's old and smells like sweat, cars, and something acrid.

Mom's nose wrinkles.

"That's gunpowder, Red. See their uniforms? This is the Army. There's nothing further from freedom than the Army. Are you sure you want to do this? You'll go God knows where with God knows whom, and you'll work your butt off. You'll never be a pet."

"What if I don't want to go?"

"Bite him, dear, like you did with that other guy who wanted you, the one who smelled like cats. Otherwise, your Army career is staring you in the face. Is this what you want?"

"How would I know?"

Mom nods.

"True that. You rejected every chance to be a pet; I don't know what else Jones can find for you."

I sniff Shorty again. He's nothing to write home about, even if I knew how to write, but he's OK. And he's lonely. I sense no kids, no wife, no pets. Just stale beer, wood smoke, and gunpowder. He needs someone to look after him.

I stare him in the eye, and he stares back. Nobody blinks.

He bursts laughing.

"She's something else, this one. We'll take her."

Jones nods. Mom's ears flatten, and she suddenly looks sad and old.

"Let's go, little girl," Shorty says, reaching for my collar.

I bare my teeth and growl. He stares at me with wide eyes.

"What's up, Baby?"

I point to Mom.

"I need to say goodbye."

He steps back.

I lick Mom's nose, pretending I don't see her shiny eyes.

"I love you, Mom. I'm sorry if I disappointed you, but I need to be who I am. I love you."

"I love you too, Red. You didn't disappoint me, just the opposite. You're just like your father, Rocky, who got wounded in Afghanistan. He earned a purple heart. He's a hero. None of my other kids turned out like him. I'm so proud of you."

"Thank you, Mom. I'll be back."

"I hope so. In my old age, I'd love to get to see my kids again. You, especially."

I lick her nose and sniff her for the last time, then I say goodbye to Jones, who's biting his lips to stop from crying. People are weird. He chose to send me away, and now he's all upset. Why? Who knows? I walk to Shorty and sit next to him. He nods.

"You're ready? Let's go then."

He opens the door. I try to jump in, but it's too high, and I fall on my face. The young whippersnapper laughs and then helps me up. His smell raises my hackles.

As we drive away, Whippy asks:

"What are we going to call her? Red?"

Shorty laughs.

"Oh, no. This beautiful young lady deserves better than that. And she's not even red, she's black and tan. Mostly black. From now on, she'll be Guinness. The queen of beers."

As we drive through the potholes, I lay my nose on my paws and think about Mom and Jones. I miss them terribly, and I know they miss me even more.

"I'll be back, Mom."

I hope that's true.

4

The training was fun. Except for obedience training, of course. Being told what to do has never been my bowl of kibble. But I liked Shorty, and I enjoyed making him happy. More importantly, I was hungry, and training came with food. Gone were the days when Jones filled my bowl with High-Performance Grass-Fed Beef kibble three times a day, not counting the buttered popcorn that came with the movies. I now had to work for my food.

My training started as soon as we got to Shorty's house, a small blue ranch at the edge of town.

I started at the front door and sniffed everything: boots, remote controls, ashtrays. The green velour sofa smelled like tobacco, beer, and Shorty. Nobody else. I moved from the kitchen to the bathroom, where I scored. The large brush behind the water bowl smelled delicious. Tasted good, too, so I lay down to brush my teeth.

"Guinness, come," Shorty called.

I was busy, so ignored him. He was welcome to come over if he needed me.

But then he shook the food container, and my stomach growled, reminding me I hadn't eaten since breakfast. So off I went.

That's how I learned to sit, stay, down, and heel. I didn't enjoy it, but as Mom said, I had rejected every chance to be a pet. I had to work for a living.

It wasn't all work, though. We took long walks every morning, though Shorty needed a lot of encouragement. It wasn't his fault. He's missing his front legs, so he had to walk on his hind paws all the time. It was hard to watch, really, but he did a good job, considering. After training, we stretched on the sofa, drank Bud Light, and watched action movies. That's how I learned to appreciate beer. Shorty poured a few drops in my dish every time he opened a can. At first, I tried it just to be polite, but then I got into it. I liked the way it tickled my tongue. So did Shorty. By bedtime, he'd slur his commands, but it didn't matter, since I had learned to hear his thoughts. He still spoke a lot.

One evening he showed me the picture of a stiff couple staring straight into the camera. Dressed in black and unsmiling, they looked like they'd never chewed on a juicy bone or tried a good mud bath. But Shorty's eyes got wet.

"This is my mother."

His mother didn't look anything like my mom. She had cold eyes and a thin mouth. Even worse, she had no tail; but then neither did Shorty. It must be genetic.

"And this is Dad."

Shorty choked up and blew his nose in the kitchen towel.

"When I was a kid, he used to take me clamming in Maine. We'd go camping there every summer and look for clams in the mud. I've still got his clamming fork. Let me show you."

He came back from the garage with a short pitchfork with ugly flat teeth.

"Isn't she beautiful? Forty years later, and she's still as good as new. Have you ever seen anything like it?"

I hadn't really, and I was doing just fine, but I slapped my tail on the floor to be polite. The last thing I wanted was to hurt Shorty's feelings.

"Guess what, Guinness? We're going clamming."

That sounded interesting. I'd never seen clams before, but I knew mud, and I loved it. I still do. The rotten eggs smell. The way it farts as it squishes between your toes! And the lovely coating that spikes your fur! I was all in.

We loaded the Jeep with food, a tent, and a stinky gas stove. I sniffed everything and knocked down a thing or two, getting in Shorty's way at every step to slow him down and help him make good choices.

We started north before sunrise. The sun went up, then back down, as we munched on chips and listened to the radio where dude after dude complained about their cheating females and their old trucks breaking down. I wondered about cheating. Is it like when Black tried to steal my food? I had an easy fix for that. I just bared my teeth and growled, and he left me alone. I wanted to ask Shorty, but he was busy singing along in his creaky voice.

"I love country music. It keeps me going on long rides and reminds me how good I've got it."

And a long ride it was. By the time we got there, it was too dark for clamming. We put up the tent, drank beer, ate Bush's beans, and watched the stars blinking up above. Shorty loved them.

"See, Guinness, when we die, our soul becomes a star. It looks down upon Earth and waits for our loved ones to come and join us. I know Father's there; I just don't know which one he is. When I die, I'll join him, and we'll go clamming together again."

I sniffed them looking for Shorty 's father, but they were too far and too many. I smelled nothing but the beans, the seaweed, and Shorty's socks.

"See that shiny one there? That's the North Star. It shows you the north. It will help you get home if you ever get lost."

He started explaining how I can find it by adding five times the distance between these two stars to the direction of those other two. At first I thought he was kidding, but nope, he was darn serious. Smart humans can say the most amazing things. Watch the stars?

How about following your nose? I can't even walk while staring up at the sky. Humans!

We slept in the tent, keeping each other warm, then walked to the beach at sunrise. The tide had covered the sand with sea creatures entangled in garlands of green seaweed. I don't do greens, but I found two small crabs and a tiny silver fish. The sand coating gave them a satisfying crunch. I found another fish for Shorty, but he was busy digging in the mud, so I ate that one too.

Sweat ran down Shorty's face as he dug with his pitchfork. He looked exhausted. Time to help him, I thought. Before you could say kibble bits, I dug a hole as big as our tent, and I called him over. He shook his head.

"There are no clams there, Guinness. That's way too deep. We don't dig for the sake of digging. We look for clams, you see?"

He showed me a sandy rock that smelled like the sea.

OK then. I brought Shorty a rock even bigger than his, but he laughed and threw it away. I got it back, but he ignored it and kept digging.

When he was done, he covered his clams with seaweed to keep them moist though he didn't need to. We walked to the tent in an icy drizzle that seeped into our bones and made us shiver. If those clams could shiver, they would have. But Shorty made a fire, and we warmed up, drinking beer while waiting for the water to boil.

As always after a few sips, he started talking.

"I've been with the Army for thirty years, Guinness. Good years. I bought a house and paid off my mortgage; I even set aside a little money. Father would be so proud of me. I wish I could tell him. I think about him every day, but here, up north, I feel him with me."

His voice cracks. I lay my head on his thigh, and he scratches me behind the ears.

"You know your father, Guinness? Do you miss him?"

I only know what Mom told me, and I don't miss him. How can you miss someone you never met? But I feel Shorty's pain, so I lick his beer.

He laughs and starts cooking the clams. He brought scallions, parsley, and other useless green stuff, but he also got chorizo - a sausage with an attitude.

He pours them all over the clams, then sprinkles over a yellow powder that makes me sneeze. He laughs.

"That's Old Bay, Guinness. Father said you can't cook seafood without Old Bay. That's what makes it real."

If you say so. I'd be just fine with just the chorizo, but who am I to disagree with Shorty's father?

That evening we ate clams, we drank beer, and listened to country music. Shorty was happy and pleased with himself, and I didn't want to hurt his feelings. But those clams? They smelled like Old Bay, and they had more sand than the fish I found on the beach.

In the morning we packed up and went home. I had a splendid time. I just wish I could tell my Mom that I found a good home after all.

5

I woke up one morning to discover that the world had turned white. I couldn't believe it.

Nothing but white everywhere. Blanketing the ground, outlining the trees, covering the house. More white kept falling from the sky. I opened my mouth to catch it, but it vanished. It was soft and so cold it felt hot. The world was white and quiet.

That filled me with so much joy that I needed to jump out of my skin. I loved that white, and I wanted it all. I rolled in it, I dug into it, I ate it. I was in love.

Shorty watched me from the door, his thin hair messed up from sleep, his smile cracking his face from one ear to the other.

"You like it, huh? It's snow."

He bent over and picked some, molded it into a ball, and threw it at me. I jumped to catch it, but it disappeared amongst the whiteness. He threw another. This time I got it, but it was like grabbing the wind. I chomped on it, and it disappeared.

He laughed and threw another, then another. I leaped to catch them, sliding and falling and jumping again. I'd never had so much fun.

"You know what, Guinness? How about we skip training today, and we take a snow day. What do you think?"

"Seriously?"

"Yep."

I leaped and barked with joy. He put on his boots and his coat, then came to play with me. His face turned pink with cold, but his eyes warmed with laughter. I'd never seen him happier. Before long, we'd flattened the snow and turned it from fluffy to slippery. Running got tricky.

I was just gathering myself after a face-plant when a green Cadillac stopped by the driveway, and Shorty's smile vanished like the snow I'd chomped on.

The driver was a woman, old, crooked and unsmiling. I went to greet her, since she looked familiar, but she ignored me. Her fierce eyes were glued on Shorty.

"Hello, Mother."

"Hello, Alfred."

She stared at him. He stared back. She had his narrow down-turned eyes, but she lacked his warmth and his softness.

"I came for the last time."

"I see."

"I had to. God reminded me that he will take me soon, but I have to finish my work here first. I can't go to Him without giving it one more try."

"I'm sorry you bothered, Mother. Especially in a snowstorm."

She leaned toward him, her hands on her hips, her voice thunder.

"Alfred, it's not too late to renounce your evil ways and turn your heart back to God. He'll take you back to His flock if you repent."

"Repent for what?"

"You know that better than I do."

"Mother, I've got nothing for you. I believe, and I pray, and I do my best to hurt nobody and be the best man I can be. There's little else I can do, for God or for you."

"You're not a man. You know what you are."

"I am what I am because God made me this way. I didn't ask for it."

"My only son. An abomination. Refusing to see the sin of his ways. Refusing to repent. What did I ever do to deserve this?"

"Good question, Mom. Now, if you'll excuse me, I have work to do."

"Work? You're just playing with that filthy dog. So, you refuse to answer God's call, repent, and become a faithful man."

"Mother, I am a faithful man. And she's not a filthy dog. Her name is Guinness. She's the best K-9 I ever had the privilege to train. Now, if you'll excuse us..."

The woman spits in the snow, and that drives me nuts. I don't spit—I drool, and I occasionally puke when I eat the wrong thing—but I know what spitting means. She's disrespecting Shorty, just like a dog who'd pee in my territory to show me that I don't matter. This is Shorty's home, and this woman has no business being rude. I get that, even though I don't understand her words.

She raises her fist in the air.

"You are an abomination. God..."

I'm done with this nonsense. That's enough. This woman will not disrespect Shorty while he's in my care. I growl, bare my teeth, and lunge at her.

"Gather your nonsense and go away. Now!"

Her stare moves from Shorty to me. I get in her face, close enough to get her in one leap, and bark out a storm. Her eyes widen.

She's scared. Good. That's the idea. Get out of here, lady, and leave my Shorty alone.

"Alfred!"

I bark even louder to drown Shorty's voice calling me back. Obedience is one thing; responsibility is another. Shorty is my responsibility. He's my human, and I won't let anyone hurt him, not even his mother.

I'm about to take a bite of her flowing black skirts, just to clarify my message, when she climbs back in her Cadillac and slams the door shut. She takes off, blowing a cloud of snow behind her. I don't blink until she's out of sight.

I turn back to see Shorty's as white as the snow. The joy drained out of him like the air out of a spiked balloon. He looks old, sad, and frail. I know he'll tell me off for ignoring his order, but I don't care. It was for his own good. That's what we, dogs, are here for. To protect our humans whether they like it or not. I won't obey an order that could hurt my human. But he says nothing, and I feel bad.

"Sorry, Shorty. I just tried to help."

We go back in. He takes off his coat, shedding snow all over the linoleum floor, then pours me a bowl of kibble.

"Thanks for getting her off my back, Guinness. You made it easier."

Seriously? He's totally deflated. Easy is not what comes to mind. But, little by little, he gathers some color. By the time I finish breakfast, he's back to being himself.

"That was my mother, you know. She never got used to who I

am, and she couldn't stand that Father loved me anyhow. They separated when I was just a teenager. She didn't want me, so she left me with Dad, but she never gave up. Every once in a while, she still comes back to remind me that I'm a useless failure and that God hates me."

I don't get that. I don't know God, but I don't see anything wrong with Shorty. He's my favorite human ever. I love him even better than I loved Jones. Jones was Mom's human, and I just got to tag along. Shorty is mine and only mine. And he's terrific, baldness and beer and all.

"I tried to be the best person I could be, but that wasn't enough for her. I can't be who she wants me to be: A family man with a wife and children, reading the Bible in church every Sunday. But that's not me. I'm lucky to have the Army for a family. And you. I've never seen anyone silence Mother before. Not even Father. I think I'll keep you around."

As I go to take a nap, I wonder at how strange humans are. Mom accepted me as I was, even though I wasn't who she expected me to be. She loved me just the same. What's wrong with humans? What can't they love each other as they are? I don't get it.

I love Shorty even when he snores, farts, and makes no sense. That's what love is all about, isn't it?

6

After obedience, we moved to combat training. That was so much fun! I got to bark, bite, and fight boogeymen all day long. I woke up every day looking forward to my training. I didn't want it to end.

Shorty was glad to see me so excited about learning. Still, he never failed to remind me that combat is more than physical. It's a calling.

"What you do matters, Guinness. You aren't a pet to lay around, watch TV, and eat snacks all day long. You are a professional and an officer. Your mission is to keep the good guys safe and lock away the bad guys. Be proud of your work and give it all you've got."

So I did.

We trained in an enormous hangar full of tools: rock-filled plastic jugs sounding like explosions when they hit the floor; leather rags; treadmills, and deafening whips louder than gunshots. My favorite was the bite trainer, but I'm getting ahead of myself.

Training K-9s for combat starts with building frustration and bite work. You'd think biting is easy since you've been doing it since you grew teeth. But a professional K-9 bite is nothing like eating Jones's boots or even like chewing on the cat. Professional biting is a complex skill that takes work to master. Here's a mini-tutorial if you want to try it:

#1. Don't bite with your incisors, your front teeth, nor on one side. Bite with your molars, the big teeth at the back of your mouth.

#2. Fill your whole mouth with whatever you're biting, whether it's a rag, a bite pillow, or a perpetrator (that's what we call the bad guys).

#3. When you bite, push forward to grip deeper instead of pulling away. Your incisors will rip and shred, allowing the perpetrator to escape, while your molars will crush and hold the prey.

#4. Never let go.

It may sound easy, but Shorty and I spent weeks and weeks on my bite work. We started with a leather rag, then moved on to the leather pillow. Never burlap. Why, you ask? Because wet leather gets slippery, forcing you to tighten your grip. That's how you build champions, Shorty said.

Once he was happy with my bite and grip, we started training on the bite sleeve—leather too, of course. Shorty put it on above his clothes to teach me to target my bite on the perp's arm and hold on to it. Once I learned that, he started screaming, shouting, and trying to shake me off. He even cracked the whip above my head to make me let go. Are you kidding? I bit even deeper and held on for dear life. The best game ever!

After I got good with the sleeve, we moved on to the boogeymen. They're decoys wearing thick padded suits who pretend to be perpetrators. They appear out of nowhere and threaten you. Your job is to grab them, pull them down, and hold them there until your handler pulls you off.

But I didn't know that until the day Whippy came to help with the training. Shorty drove us to the forest.

"The boogeyman is where you separate the grain from the chaff. No matter how you check the dog's breeding and test their environmentals, you may still get surprised."

"What are environmentals?" Whippy asked.

"The dog's response to whatever happens around him. Some dogs get scared and back up. Some get mad and push forward. You won't know which is which until you try."

"Why?"

"When a dog faces a threatening challenge he's never seen before, he has no learning to support him. He only has his instinct and the genes he inherited from his ancestors. You won't know what those are until you try them."

"Are you saying she'll fail?"

"Of course not. Guinness will pass with flying colors. I'm not so sure about you."

Whippy snickered and left, then Shorty and I took a walk and fell upon the boogeyman threatening us with a whip.

I started barking like I'd seen a cat and leaped forward, dragging Shorty on his leash, but the boogeyman disappeared in the bushes.

"Good girl, Guinness. Nice job."

"Not really. The creep escaped," I growled. I rose my hackles to look scarier, and I sniffed along the bushes looking for the boogeyman, but he'd vanished. I stayed on high alert though, and when he returned, I was ready.

I leaped and caught him. I filled my mouth with his arm, biting hard, and grabbed him with my legs to pull him closer. I'd give my tail for opposable thumbs, I thought, as I crushed his arm through the padded suit and pulled him to the ground.

"Jesus," the boogeyman gasped.

The smell of onions confirmed what I knew: the boogeyman was Whippy. I growled like a Harley Davidson with a broken muffler and bit even deeper.

He lashed me with the whip, and the pain took my breath away, but I didn't let go. He hit me again. My left ear was on fire, but I bit even deeper.

"Don't hurt her, you moron," Shorty shouted. "You're not

supposed to hit her, just to make noise and scare her, then pull away."

Whippy didn't listen. He slammed his whip against my head again, then kneed me in the throat, but I didn't let go. When I felt his imbalance, I pulled him to the ground, then jumped on him and kept him there.

Shorty pulled me up by the choke collar until I could no longer breathe, and I had to let go. I sat panting by his side as he checked on Whippy.

"Are you hurt?"

Whippy stood up and spat to the side, but he was okay. I never tasted blood, and that padded suit wouldn't let my canines go through.

My ears were on fire though. I cried when Shorty touched them. Even worse, I couldn't reach to lick them, no matter how hard I stuck my tongue out.

We drove back home in silence. Shorty sent me inside and closed the door.

"Why did you hit her?"

"I had to defend myself."

"No, you didn't. This is not what you do. Your job is to teach the dog and build her confidence, not to hurt her. I thought even you knew that much!"

"It's nothing but a bruise. She'll be better in no time, looking forward to the next session."

"She might, but you won't. I'm done with you. Find yourself another trainer."

"Are you kidding?"

"No. I don't want you near my dog ever again."

"You can't train her by yourself."

"That's none of your business. Get lost."

Whippy left. Shorty and I split a beer, and as always, he started talking.

"I'm sorry your ears hurt, Guinness. That won't happen again. There, this helps."

He got some ice cubes in a plastic bag and put them on my head.

I ate them as soon as he looked away. I love ice cubes—they're cold, slippery, and crunchy. I spat out the bag.

"What a loser, to find joy in hurting those weaker than him."

"I beg your pardon?"

"You're still a pup, Guinness, and you still have a lot to learn. That's what I'm here for. To make you into the best K-9 you can be. Someday you'll save somebody's life."

That would be nice. In the meantime, however, I'd like to kill Whippy. I don't think anyone will miss him.

7

Shorty said I graduated combat training with flying colors. I looked everywhere, but nothing was flying but the crow I'd chased from the bushes, and he was black.

Shorty laughed.

"You're a big girl now, Guinness. Time to look for a job. What would you like to do?"

I hate that question. That's what Mom asked before I joined the Army, a lifetime ago when I was just a puppy. Now I'm a real German shepherd. Nobody ow-oohs over me and rushes to pet me, even though I'm beautiful, Shorty says. My best feature is my tail— long, shiny, and expressive, just like Mom's. That's how I talk to Shorty. That, and my ears. I can't imagine how people can make it through life without tails. Even cats have them, for dog's sake, though they use them all wrong. Instead of wagging their tails when they're happy, they wag them when they're mad. No wonder we don't get along. But I digress.

"Can we go places?"

"We could, but we won't be going to many fun places. We'd go to danger zones where life is hard, and death stares at you from everywhere. We may never come back."

"Bummer."

"On the other hand, you've already aced obedience, tracking, and apprehension. You could further your training and learn to detect explosives. After that, you'd be an MPC, Multi-Purpose Canine. The best-trained dogs ever."

"I'd like that."

"I'll put in an application. I think they'll take us since there's a desperate need for explosive detecting canines. We need them everywhere: in the Army to protect our troops, in police work, at the border, and for TSA to look for bombs and firearms. When they see your record, they'll beg us to join. We should find out in a week or two."

But we didn't have a week or two.

The phone rang in the middle of the night. At first, I thought I was dreaming, since the phone never rings in Shorty's house. His voice was thick with sleep when he answered.

"What?"

He sat up and glanced at me.

"Of course, she's here. Where else could she be?"

We were alone, so I knew he was talking about me. Cool! I never get phone calls, I thought. Who would call me? Then my heart skipped a beat. Did something happen to Mom?

"When? Yesterday? So why didn't you call us then?"

I crawl closer to listen in, but I hear nothing.

"Where?"

Silence.

I miss Mom. Her warm tongue licking away my sorrows, her amber eyes looking into my soul, her wisdom, her love. I seldom thought of her when I was training, but the thought she may be in trouble breaks my heart.

"We'll be there in an hour."

"An hour? Why an hour? Why not now?"

Shorty hangs up and looks at me.

"Your first mission, Guinness. A little girl disappeared last night.

Her mom put her to bed, but she was gone in the morning. Nobody knows what happened. Did she wander out and get lost, or did someone take her? You need to find her."

Me? But I don't do kids! They scream, pull your tail, and stick their fingers in your mouth, and you're supposed to think they're cute! Poppycock! They're just untrained human puppies, but you can't even growl to tell them off, let alone bite them!

Shorty opens the door to send me out as he gets dressed. My hackles are up, and my legs tremble. I'm terrified. As I pee on the bushes, I consider running away. This is too much and too fast. A kid? Really?

I can make it to the forest. Shorty can't catch me. He's improved since I've been training him, but he's old, and he only has two legs. I could live on grass and whatever grows on trees. Bacon maybe?

But I remember what Shorty said about my mission. I trained all this time to save a life someday. Is today someday?

I drag my tail back inside. Shorty's all kitted-up with his helmet and his body armor. He slips my armored vest over my head and buckles it, then starts the Jeep, and I jump in. My heart races. For the first time in my life, I'm scared.

Our lights break a tunnel in the darkness as Shorty drives faster than he should. I smell his excitement and fear, and I feel better knowing that he's scared too.

"That's not how I thought your first job would go, Guinness. But it is what it is. Technically, this is not our problem, but the police folks asked for our help. Apparently, their Malinois isn't getting anywhere."

I sit up a little. There now. Wouldn't that be fun to show this Malinois a thing or two! And save the kid, of course.

"Her parents put her to bed at eight. This morning she was gone. The doors weren't locked—it's that kind of neighborhood. Police have been looking and got nothing. The odds of finding her alive drop by the minute, but they wasted a day before they called us. Moronic neophytes!"

That's strong language for Shorty, who's a mild-mannered man, more into clamming than into fights. But I store that for the next time I meet a Malinois.

The pale house sits in a lovely neighborhood: tall houses surrounded by greenery, attached garages, playscapes, plenty of room to roam. The car lights find a narrow driveway flanked by trees, then the house standing like a ghost amid the turmoil. All around it, police cars blink like Christmas trees. Lights are on everywhere; the whole neighborhood is awake and watching.

Shorty parks outside the yellow tape and shows his ID to the uniforms guarding the entrance. They let us through as cameras flash and people shout questions. They all look forward to seeing us at work, and I choke with fear. I so wish I knew what I'm doing.

8

With its gleaming floors and tall windows, the house would be lovely if it weren't for the yellow tape across the doors, the people crawling all over to get samples, and the smell of doom.

The odor doesn't come from the house. It comes from the people. To dogs, people smell like they feel: happy, anxious, angry, or scared. Every one of these people works feverishly and sweats fear, and the scent of doom is so thick it chokes me.

Shorty stops in front of a wide uniformed man, whose shoulders are heavy with shiny things, and salutes. The man's neither young nor good-looking, but he exudes authority. Even I can feel it, and I don't give a hoot about authority.

"Thanks for coming, Shorty. I wish they called you sooner."

"So do I, Colonel. This is Guinness, my partner."

"She looks young."

"She is. This is her first mission."

"I see. Well, we can only do the best we can."

Shorty's jaw clenches so hard that I can see the little muscle twitching.

"Which way?"

The man points to the stairs.

"Go, Guinness."

I sniff my way up the stairs, stopping on every step. I've never looked for a person before. I only tracked widgets. You know, the round metal things that go on screws? Shorty taught me how to follow them by their smell. The day I found every single one, he gave me a whole bag of buttered popcorn. Boy, what cramps I had that night! And then diarrhea. And it wasn't pink and sweet-smelling like that time I ate a whole bar of soap. This one was brown and smelled like poop.

After a few steps, I get in a groove. I gain momentum and accelerate, dragging Shorty behind me. He's panting, but he keeps the pace, and we get to the second floor. As I sniff, odors flow through my nostrils into my brain, where they flash like the images from a movie trailer. Old sneakers. Orange. Bubble gum. Baby shampoo.

I turn right. This is the girl's room: An army of stuffed animals; pink walls with unicorns jumping over rainbows. I sniff the pink carpet, the tiny shoes, and the ruffly dress crumpled on the pink armchair. Painfully pink, I think, and I move on to the wardrobe.

A black K-9 in a bulletproof vest stares at me from behind the mirror. I bare my teeth—he does the same. I growl—he growls back. I sniff him. He smells like baby shampoo. What a sissy, I think, and move on to the open window.

Something's different here. New odors of onions, sweat, and fear float in from the old oak tree by the window. There may be ten feet to the ground, but the tree is easy to scale. Even I could do it, and I don't have opposable thumbs.

I glance back. Shorty stands at the other end of the leash, his burning eyes glued on me.

I sit, giving the signal. He unhooks the leash.

"Go."

I leap out the window onto a thick branch, eight feet from the ground. I lose my balance, but I hang on and crawl down the fork to the trunk, where I sniff the onions again. I creep to a lower branch, thankful for all those times Shorty had me walk the narrow plank in agility training, then jump to the ground. I hope Shorty can follow, despite his leg shortage. But whether he does or he doesn't, I have to do what I have to do. I track the scent across the lawn, then through the garden to the forest, sniffing at every step. By now, I'm making good progress, so I speed up, and I leap down the path, stopping to sniff every once in a while.

Oops! The trail's gone. I lost the scent. There's nothing left. It's like whoever was here just flew away. Jeepers!

I turn around and head back, looking for where I lost the trail, but I can't find it. It disappeared. I'm thinking about returning to the house and starting over when I recover the track where the path nears the stream. They must have crossed here.

Sure enough, I pick up the scent on the other side. It's stronger now. I glance back for Shorty, but he's nowhere to be seen. I lost him somewhere, but I have no time to wait. I run down the narrow path between the trees, farther and farther. I see a glimmer of light, and I reach a small cottage. The lights are still on, even though it's got to be almost tomorrow.

I peek through the window—a small room with a table, a narrow bed, and some chairs. And there's my girl.

She sits in a highchair, her pink pajamas sprinkled with cloudy sheep, her cheeks wet with tears, staring at the banana in front of her.

The fat man next to her leans against the table to touch her cheek. She shivers.

"Eat your banana."

"I don't want it. I want my mommy. When can I go home to my mommy?"

"Very soon, if you're a good girl."

"I'm a good girl. I want my mommy."

"Then eat your banana. There, try that."

He sprays a cloud of whipped cream on the banana and brings it to her mouth. She licks it.

"Good girl."

He traces her wet cheeks with his finger, then dips it in whipped cream and holds it to her mouth. She licks it off, and he starts panting like he's been running. He kisses her hair, then her forehead, then her mouth, as her eyes grow wide and scared. He smells like fear, onions, and something else. It's like he's in heat.

"I have something better than that banana for you."

I don't know what that is, but I feel I can't wait anymore. I must go in now.

But I can't!

I've never done this before. I never fought a perpetrator, just the boogeymen. And never alone. I can't do this without Shorty.

What if I went back to get him? He'll never find me otherwise. I'll just get him and return. I look back. Nothing but silent darkness, but I'll follow my nose and find my way.

I head back to get Shorty.

The girl screams.

9

He's trying to take off her pajamas, and she won't let him.

He slaps her, and she screams a blood-curdling cry of terror like I've never heard before. I shiver, my heart pounds, and my brain catches fire.

I'm all alone, and I've never done this before. I can't do it. I need to get Shorty right now.

That's the last thing I remember before I blow through the window and grab onto his arm.

He squeals like a pig and lets go of the girl to punch me in the nose. He sticks his fingers in my eyes, and I wish I could bite and break them, but I can't. I can't let go of his arm.

The girl screams. I'd like to tell her not to worry. I've got it. She's all right now that I'm here. But I can only growl, since my mouth is full of the man's thick arm. Every time he moves, I bite harder, like Shorty taught me.

Now what? What do I do? Where's Shorty? He was supposed to be here and get me off him!

The man punches me again and again, but I won't let go. I hang on to his arm with all my weight, trying to pull him to the ground, but he holds on to the table and leans over to grab a knife.

I clutch onto the ground with my claws and pull back, struggling to drag him away, but he's too heavy.

He lifts the knife and plunges it to stab me in the chest. I'm ready for pain, but the blade can't cut through my bulletproof vest, and it feels just like another punch. I bite even deeper.

I taste his blood as he lifts the knife again. This time a searing pain in my hip takes my breath away, since my vest doesn't cover my legs. He sees me flinch, and lifts the knife again. The pain is so sharp that it sets my paw on fire. I slip off his arm and crash to the ground.

He leans over me, his bloody knife ready. An evil grin splits his ugly face as he lifts the blade. I roll over, then leap and grab onto his throat. He drops the knife and falls to the ground.

I hold on to my bite and jump on his chest. He starts snoring, and I can't believe he fell asleep while we're fighting. He's got to be faking it. I get ready to bite deeper.

"Let go, Guinness. I've got him."

Shorty's words come out clipped with his ragged breath. He must have run all the way here. Boy, am I proud of him!

"Are you sure?" I growl.

"Yep."

I let go. The man doesn't move. As he lies snoring on the floor, I limp to the girl in pink pajamas. Streaks of tears cut through the whipped cream on her cheeks, but her face lights up into a smile.

"Hey, it's all good, baby. You're going home."

"Doggy?"

"Sort of. I prefer being called a K-9. It's more respectful, you know."

"Doggy!"

Oh well. I get close enough to lick the whipped cream off her cheeks, but I don't touch the banana. I hate bananas.

"Great job, Guinness." Shorty puts away his weapon, then kneels to check my wounds as two uniforms handcuff the fat man, then take him away on a stretcher.

"Nothing major, Guinness. Just flesh wounds. I bet you won't even need stitches. I'm so proud of you!"

"Thanks. Can we go home now?"

"Soon."

It turns out he lied. It took hours and hours of talking to the officers, then waiting for the photographers to take pictures. The little girl was long gone by then. She cried when her mommy took her away.

"Doggy, Doggy."

"That's all right, Rose. We'll get you a puppy."

"Doggy?"

Shorty and I were left behind to deal with the mess.

"Good work, Guinness. You too, Shorty," the colonel said. He shook Shorty's hand, then offered me some peppered beef jerky.

"Thanks, Colonel. We can only do the best we can."

The colonel laughed.

"Your best wasn't too shabby. I think the girl will be alright. Guinness got here just in time."

"How about the perpetrator?"

"The EMT's think that he'll make it too, though he won't be singing anytime soon."

"Good."

"He's got a history. He's done some time for attempting to kidnap a kid a few years ago. They just let him go last month. This time they'll throw away the key."

What key? And why would you throw it away? What if you need it later? But I have no more energy left to think about some useless key. I'm hungry and thirsty, and my wounds hurt. Even Shorty, who never complains, looks exhausted. His face is ashen and his hands shake as he cleans my cuts.

"Looking good, Guinness. Thank God it wasn't much of a knife. By tomorrow, you'll be as good as new. Good job, partner."

The sun is up by the time he drags himself to bed. No wonder he wouldn't wake up.

10

It got dark again by the time I woke up. I was desperate to pee, and my belly growled. I needed food, but I didn't want to be rude. Shorty had a long day for a human. He needed his rest.

I waited and waited until I couldn't wait anymore. I went to wake him up.

He lay motionless, staring at the ceiling. I whined, but he didn't move. I barked, but he didn't blink. I licked his hand. It was cold and stiff, and it smelled funky. That's how I knew he was dead. He smelled just like Whiskey, Jones's cat.

That tabby was the worst feline I ever met. He was bigger than me and acted like I didn't belong in Jones's home. Never a nice word or a polite greeting. No matter how gently I jumped on him to invite him to play, he'd fluff himself like a striped toilet brush and hiss, moan, and try to scratch my eyes out.

"He's deaf, dear," Mom said. "He didn't hear you say good morning. When you touched him, he thought you crept behind to scare him."

"What an ice-hole," I said, licking my bloody lip.

Mom gasped.

"Red! Where did you learn this kind of vocabulary?"

I hung my head, flattened my ears, and did my best to look contrite, but she wouldn't relent.

"Where did you hear this? I want to know."

Like really? Where do you think I did? Where do I ever go by myself? Nowhere, ever. Even at the dog park you watch my every move. I learned it at home, of course.

"From Jones."

Mom sits up straight and crinkles her nose to bare her teeth like she does whenever Jones invites her for a bath. She's not crazy about baths, Mom, even though she never hesitates to give me one. But there's something about shampoo that raises her hackles.

"That's not true, Red. Do you know what we call people who say things that are not true?"

"Malinois?"

If you're a German shepherd, being called a Malinois is the worst insult. Everybody knows they are fickle and neurotic. Even

Mom. Whenever we misbehaved, she'd growl at us: "Don't act like a Malinois."

Not today. She snorts, and I lie my nose on my paws, doing my best to look repentant. I hope she'll get over it, but no. She's on a roll. I love Mom dearly, but I wish she wouldn't get into these funks. She's got this thing about good manners, especially for the girls. She'd do anything to make an exemplary young lady out of me. Not gonna happen, Mom. Not to me.

"Those who don't tell the truth are liars. And that's an insult. You don't ever want to hear that from anyone. Never. Got it, Red?"

I give up. I roll on my back, presenting my belly in submission. Mom gathers her tail and stomps out, looking dignified, but I bet you she went out to chill. Because deep inside, she knows I'm not lying.

Whenever Jones watches sports, Mom takes off somewhere for a beauty nap. She finds sports noisy and boring. That's when Jones shouts things unsuitable for a lady's ears. He agitates, sputters, and hollers at the fat people playing ball with some sticks as they trample all over each other.

"JD, you lousy piece of crap. You could catch that one if you got off your butt, but no. You lazy fudge!" Except he didn't say "crap" or "fudge."

I didn't watch the TV. I watched him, storing every word for future use. That's where I learned the stuff Mom disapproves of.

But we were talking about Whiskey.

One morning, Jones came out of his bedroom, his eyes red and swollen, his voice broken like the dinner plate I ate the other day. I grabbed a stick and went to cheer him up, but Mom pulled me aside.

"Let him be, Red."

"Why? What's up with him?"

"He's upset. His old buddy Whiskey died."

"How?"

"I don't know. Whiskey was a nasty old coot, really, but he was

Jones's best friend, and Jones is heartbroken. He needs time to mourn."

"Why?"

"Because he'll never play with him again, hear him purr, or curl with him for a nap. That's so sad."

That sounded like excellent news to me, but people are weird. I snuck into the bedroom to check out Whiskey. He laid on his pillow as usual, staring at me with wide-open yellow eyes. I talked to him, but he wouldn't answer. Like, what's new? I went closer to sniff him. He was cold, stiff, and smelled funky. Just like Shorty.

Mom sighed.

"That's the smell of death, Red dear. Everybody dies sooner or later."

"What happens when they die?"

"I don't know. People think they'll go somewhere warm, green, and peaceful. Like an all-inclusive resort where you get together with all those you loved and lost. God is supposed to make the bookings."

"Is that true?"

"I don't know, Red, but I'd be surprised. There's no such thing as a free lunch, let alone a free, all-inclusive vacation. Moreover, I wonder why nobody ever comes back. Can it really be that good? And the funny part is that they don't even take their bodies with them. The body stays here to get burned or buried. Like really? Without a body, how can you eat, run, and have fun? You don't even have a tail to wag!"

No tail? That's awful. I hope they're wrong.

"What do you really think happens, Mom?"

"I don't know, baby. I'd love to think we'll all get together to chase squirrels and howl at the moon someday, but I doubt it. I don't think there's anything left. When you die, you die, and it's over."

I went back to smell Whiskey. I looked in his eyes, stepped on his toes, and bit his ear. He didn't even hiss. He was gone.

Jones sniffed as he dug a hole under the old pine tree. He wrapped Whiskey and his toys in his bed, placed him in the hole, and covered him with dirt.

I watched. Mother watched me watch him.

"Don't dig him out,Red."

"Why not?"

"Do you want him back?"

"No."

"So why dig him out?"

Mom was right, as always. I didn't dig out Whiskey, and he never came back.

But Shorty was different. I wanted him back. I wanted our evenings, our beer, and our clamming. I decided I'd dig him out, wherever they put him. But I couldn't. When people came to take him away, they locked me in a cage and left me there. I waited and waited, but nobody came to free me. I was sad and bored, and I needed to pee, so I started barking and wouldn't stop until some woman came.

"What?"

"Can you tell me where they took Shorty?"

She left and came back with a bowl of water and some food.

"There."

"Thanks, ma'am, but that's not what I asked. This is not about food; it's about Shorty. I need to dig him out. Where is he?"

She shrugged and left.

I lay in my cage, waiting, like forever. Nothing happened until Whippy, Shorty's former sidekick, came to see me. For the first time in my life, I was glad to see him.

"Where's Shorty?"

"Sorry, Guinness. Shorty's dead. He won't be back."

He didn't look sorry. He looked pleased, if anything. I felt my hackles rising, but I kept my voice low and sweet.

"I know that, you twit. Mom taught me long ago. Where is he, please?"

"You and me, we'll work together."

"Work together at what? Do you even know how to dig?"

"You're ready for the next stage of your training. I'll make sure you do a great job."

I sighed. I wanted to rip off Whippy's throat, right there and then, but I was in the crate, and he was out. And if I killed him, how would I find Shorty to dig him out?

I put my nose on my paws and thought of what Mom said. I so hope she was wrong. I hope Shorty is someplace green and peaceful, clamming with his father. I hope he told him about paying off his mortgage, whatever that means, and about how the two of us saved a little girl. But somehow, I don't think so.

11

If you think being a K-9 is glamorous, think again. The gunfights and the exciting apprehensions only happen in the movies. K-9 life is all about training, training, and more training. I spent day after day looking for explosives, from fertilizer to old-fashioned TNT and new plastics. Honestly, it isn't all that it's cracked up to be. I'd rather look for a burger, a bone, or even a ball, but for some strange reason, all the ATF folks look for are explosives.

But it wasn't all bad. The best part about it was that the Army took Whippy off my back. He wasn't happy.

"But Colonel, I recruited her, then trained her alongside Shorty. Now that he's gone, I'm the only person she trusts. Any other handler would have to start over. Get acquainted with her. Gain her confidence. Build a relationship."

I wonder what he's thinking. I haven't seen him since he was the boogeyman and whipped my ears. And that's too much.

The colonel is the same guy who ran the search that night we looked for the little girl. It feels like a lifetime ago. I wonder if he's got any beef jerky left. Even more, I hope he can see through Whippy's lies.

The colonel shakes his head.

"Hogwash. You aren't qualified to handle her, nor do you have the skills. She's just a puppy, but she's already too smart for you. And she's stubborn as a mule. In a couple of months, she'll tell you exactly what to do with yourself."

"But sir…"

"No but. She'll work with Silver."

Silver? Why not gold, I think, but I don't have time to wonder. The colonel dismisses Whippy and makes a phone call. He then comes to me, pats my head, and slips me a strip of jerky. I'm still drooling when someone knocks at the door.

"Bridget Silver, sir."

"Come in, Bridge. Meet your new partner."

The slight brown woman studies me from my ears to my toes with unblinking dark eyes. She's small and neat, and her dark hair sticks tight to her head. Her uniform is pressed, unlike Shorty's, which always looked like he slept in it. I sniff her. She smells odd, like she's frozen.

"I didn't request a partner, sir."

"I know. You got one anyhow."

"May I ask why?"

"This K-9 lost her handler a few days ago, just as she finished combat training. Shorty was a good man and a great handler, but the stress was too much for his heart. He died the day after their first mission. This K-9 is green but very talented. She has a lot of potential as an explosive detecting K-9. I can't think of anyone better to handle her than you."

"But sir…"

"Bridge, she needs a handler. You need a purpose. Bear died a year ago, and you're still moping. You're in the Army. We have work to do; we can't afford to mope forever. We have a country to protect, people to take care of, and enemies to put to rest. It's time you got back to work."

"But, sir, I work. I've been with Human Resources, and I…"

"I know exactly what you do, Bridge. I've watched you. You're doing the least you can do, get engaged as little as you can, and avoid any social contact to go home and mourn. It's like you're sleepwalking. That's enough. I thought I should give you a break, but that didn't help. If anything, you got worse. You'll get back in action, or you'll quit. Up to you. If the Army is no longer for you, there are other things you could do. You could garden, cook, open a doggy daycare…"

"Sir, I swore off dogs."

"Well, you'll have to swear them on again. Or quit."

I didn't understand all that, but I got the idea. That's how we, dogs, operate. We don't understand many words, but we know feelings. We smell them. I can smell fear, hate, love, anger, and guilt without even trying. Mother is even better. She can tell loneliness, pride, despair, and many others she didn't get to teach me.

Right now, I can smell Bridge's reluctance, sadness, and fear, though I don't understand it. What's she afraid of? The colonel? Getting fired? Me? She didn't blink when she met the colonel's eyes, but she avoided mine.

"You really mean it, sir?"

"I do. I care for you, Bridge, but the life you're living is no life. I won't let you bury yourself alive. I've been patient long enough, and after all this time, you're no better than you were when Bear died. Time to poop or get off the pot."

Bridge glances at me.

"How long do I have to decide?"

"A week. You take her for a partner and get back in action, or you're out."

"That's a sucky choice."

"It is. But you've squandered your other choices. And you may get a sucky choice, but not a sucky dog. This K-9 comes from champion lines. Her sire, Rocky, got a purple heart in Afghanistan. She passed basic training with flying colors. On her rooky mission, she and Shorty saved a kid when others failed. I turned down other handlers who want her. I'll have no trouble finding her a handler, but I'll have a lot of trouble finding you a better dog."

"Yes, sir."

Bridge nods and turns to me. For the first time, her black ice eyes look straight into mine.

"Let's go... What's her name?"

"Guinness. Her name is Guinness."

12

One thing is sure: Unlike Shorty, who had trouble keeping his mouth shut, Silver's not a talker. She didn't utter a single word as she drove her green Subaru out of town. The sunset glows over green fields, muddy meadows, and bubblegum-pink apple orchards. We're almost out of town when she turns in the driveway of a tiny blue house smelling like wood smoke and raccoons. She parks under an old pine and lets me out.

I leap in the tall grass and squat under the junipers. I've never been here, but I can tell junipers from far away. I like them, though they're kind of pushy. They're the kind of scent that throws itself at you and fills your nose, like garlic, dead fish, and poop. Speaking about poop: Did you know that every kind of poop smells different? They taste different too, but I won't go into that right now. I can tell horse manure from rabbit pellets, goose guano, or dog poop from a mile away. Poop is one of my areas of expertise, and I can't resist showing off. But I digress.

Silver's house is tidy and frozen, just like her. It's like nobody really lives here: clean wooden floors, gray walls, sparse furniture with nothing out of place: no lonely shoes, no scattered clothes, no open books, no leftovers. Nothing.

Silver drops her bag on the sofa and gets me a bowl of water. I slurp it down, and she brings another.

"Guinness, I hope you don't take it personally, but I can't take you."

I slap my tail on the floor.

"OK."

"I'm sure you're a great dog and all, but I'm done with dogs. I used to have a partner, you see. His name was Bear. He was more than my dog; he was my best friend. We were a team working on detecting explosives. I trained him since he was a pup. We worked, we walked, we did everything together. He was a great dog. There, that's him."

She shows me a framed picture on the wall. Silver, smiling, holding some sort of cup and a dog. He's not bad looking, with sharp dark ears, fierce eyes, and a sable coat, but there's something about him. Something's off, but I can't put my paw on it.

"This is Bear. He died last year, saving my life."

All of a sudden, the room smells like sorrow and guilt, and she looks ready to burst into tears. But she can't do it in front of me. I'm just a stranger, and she has to save face.

She blows her nose and turns to me.

"What makes it worse is that he died because of my mistake. He tried to warn me, but I didn't listen. He died to save me."

Her eyes turn red, and her face crumples like she's about to lose it, but she turns away and heads to the kitchen, where she starts opening cupboards.

"There's no dog food in the house. We could go back out to get you some, but it's hardly worth it for one night. Do you eat anything else?"

"Bacon?"

She shakes her head.

"Popcorn? Cereal? A sandwich?"

She takes out a bag of popcorn and starts the microwave, then opens a can of Labatt's. She sets the popcorn in front of me and takes a swig of beer.

I stare at her.

"Break," she says, giving me permission to eat.

I stare at her. She stares back.

"How about a little beer? I've had a stressful day."

Her lips twist into the shadow of a smile, and she pours me a little beer. I slurp it. She shakes her head and sets the popcorn on the table.

"If we share the beer, we may as well share the popcorn too."

She turns on the TV, and we watch the news. Wars. Famine. Disasters.

"That's terrible. How about a cooking show or a movie?" I ask.

She scrolls through and finds "*Homeward Bound.*"

"How's that?"

I like it, even though that cat, Sassy, is a bully. But I like Shadow and especially Chance. I can totally relate to him eating that underwear. Sadly, neither Jones's nor Shorty's looked that appetizing. By the time old Shadow limps back home, just as you thought he died in that hole, we finished the second bag of popcorn and another Labatt's, and there isn't a dry eye in the house.

She lets me out again. I sniff around to check on things, then I go bless the junipers. It's late, and the black sky is studded with more blinking stars than I can count. I sniff for Shorty's, wondering if he's up there clamming and waiting for me. Then I look for Bear. Is he waiting for Silver?

I return inside to find a folded towel by the sofa.

"This is your bed. It's not much, but it should do for one night. I'll take you back tomorrow morning."

She leaves. I curl on the towel. What will she do if the Army kicks her out? It's none of my business. She's just a stranger. All I know about her is that she drives a Subaru, drinks Labatt's, and misses a dog named Bear. I'd better worry about myself. I hope I don't end up with that loser Whippy. That thought is so depressing that I go back to thinking about Bear. What on earth was wrong with him?

Then it dawns on me. Bear wasn't a German shepherd; he was a freaking Belgian Malinois! That's what was wrong with him! Unless you have four paws and a tail, you won't know about the eternal rivalry between shepherds and Malinois. It's worse than that between the Cowboys and the Giants. We both compete for the title of being the best K-9s. There are even a few morons who think the Malinois are better, but they're wrong. Those neurotic, single-minded, high-strung Belgians lack the balance, the finesse, and the elegance of German shepherds. I'd love to show that Bear a thing or two.

I lie my nose on my paws, and I'm about to fall asleep when I hear steps next door. I jump up and bark, but it's only Silver, looking like a little girl with her tight bun undone and her Hello Kitty pajamas.

"Come," she says, getting my towel. "It's warmer in the bedroom."

I follow her, even though I'm not cold. I curl up on the towel by her bed as she gets under her blankets. I sigh and lie my nose on my paws.

Oh, Shorty, how I miss you! I can't wait to dig you out.

13

Silver didn't sleep much that night. Neither did I. She kept tossing, turning, and sniffing. I got up and looked everywhere for whatever she was sniffing for, but I couldn't find a thing. There was nothing there, I tell you. If there was anything, I'd find it since a K-9's nose is a hundred times better than a human's. There was nothing there but old sneakers, wood smoke, popcorn, and beer. I looked for Bear's scent, but it's been too long. There's no smell other than hers. It's like nobody ever comes inside this house, not even the plumber. Compared to this, Shorty's place was like a bus stop. People came in and out all the time—the UPS guy, the FedEx guy, a neighbor bringing a beer. Not here.

I wake up before sunrise, as I always do, and I watch her. After fretting the whole night, she finally fell into a restless sleep. She turns from side to side, panting like she's running. She moans, then screams:

"No, Bear. No!"

She's having a nightmare. I lick her face to make her feel better. It's salty.

"It's alright, girl. You're OK."

She opens her eyes and stares at me. For a moment, she smiles like everything's all right with the world. Then it's over.

"You aren't Bear."

You bet your assets. I'm not some neurotic Malinois, even if he's a bomb sniffer and a hero and all that. I'm Guinness Van Jones, German shepherd, K-9 extraordinaire.

But I don't have the heart to say that. I just lick her face once more, and that's like opening the hot water tap. She cries and cries and can't stop.

I don't know what to do. Licking her didn't help. I look away, pretending I can't hear her, but she won't stop. She carries on until my bladder's about to explode, so I walk to the door. She lets me out.

I water the bushes, then sniff around. Oops! Someone was here last night, and I know exactly who—one of these stinky black-and-white fake cats. One spray from those skunks and your nose is out of commission for days. I caught one once when I was young and didn't know any better. It was terrible. Jones washed me in tomato juice. Twice! I was red and salty, but I still stank. I was so embarrassed that I hid under the bed and wouldn't come out. Mom and Jones had to sleep in the guest bedroom for a week.

I consider going after the skunk to get sprayed. I bet you two strips of bacon against an empty bowl of kibble that I'd distract Silver from anything else. But what if she drops me off at the headquarters and I can't even use my nose to find Shorty? Not a good plan.

I stay out as long as I can. When I return, she's stopped crying and washed her face. I look for something to say, but the only thing that comes to mind is: "You've got to be crazy to get so worked up about a darn Malinois." I don't think that would help, so I just act like nothing happened.

She pours Cheerios and milk in two bowls. No sugar. Really? You can afford to gain a pound or two, lady. And so can I. Oh well. I inhale mine, then finish hers while she gets into her uniform.

We drive back the way we came: same fields, same houses, same bubblegum orchards, now basking in the morning sun. But now she's talking.

"Listen, Guinness. It's not that I don't like you or that you're not a good dog. I think you'll be a great dog someday. But I'm done with dogs. I think I'll get a cat."

I choke. Are you serious? Have you ever even met a cat? I remember that self-centered Whiskey who thought the whole world revolved around him—ill-tempered ice-hole. I sure hope he's not anywhere near Shorty when it's my turn to join him. I clear my throat.

"What an interesting idea. Cats are different."

"Yep. Unlike dogs, they don't get attached to people; they get attached to places. A cat would never die to save me."

You've got that right, sister.

"I don't know what I'll do next. I hope the colonel doesn't throw me out, but I think he will. He prides himself on being true to his word. He's not trying to be mean; he thinks he's helping, but he's wrong. The Army is my safe place where I know everybody. I know who to talk to and who to stay away from. Here I can be myself."

I don't think being herself in the Army does her any good, but what do I know? I used to think Shorty was lonely, but he had his clamming, his father looking after him, and me. Silver has nothing.

"I have a little pension. It's not enough, mind you, but it's better than nothing. I may start a nursery and grow plants. Bushes, flowers, trees. They aren't great company, but at least they won't blow up with a bomb. As for you, you'll be OK. You look great, in person and on paper. The handlers will fight for you."

That reminds me of Whippy. For the first time ever, I wonder if Mother was right. Maybe I should have chosen a lovely family to care for. But it's too late now. I belong to the Army, bless it. I'll have to handle whatever comes my way.

When we get to the headquarters, Silver parks away from the door to give me a chance to check out the bushes. I appreciate it since many humans forget. I do my thing, then we walk to the reception and wait.

Silver sits and wrings her hands. Her worried dark eyes meet mine, and I can see she's changed. If nothing else, she's no longer frozen. She looks like she'll burst into tears.

"I'm sorry, Guinness. No can do."

I lay my nose on my paws and look away. It's her loss. Anyhow, she's nothing like Shorty. No clamming, no country music, no bacon. But, even though I feel rejected, I hope she gets over her freaking Malinois someday.

"Malinois suck."

She stares at me in disbelief.

"What?"

I shrug.

"Sorry. I need to learn to keep my mouth shut. But we German shepherds don't think much of Malinois. Maybe it's professional jealousy, but I wouldn't throw my life away for a Malinois. Especially not a male. They think they hung the moon, but they're nothing but neurotic gigolos looking for their moment of fame."

Her jaw drops. I flatten my ears, and I look away in embarrassment.

"You can go in now."

I follow Silver to the office feeling like a loser. She didn't need my snarky comments, and they didn't do me any good either. But it's too late. We step into the office to find the colonel sitting behind his desk like he never left it. He glances up from his pile of papers and frowns.

"I gave you a week."

"You did. But there was no point to it, really. Might as well get it done and move on."

"I see. What's your decision?"

Silver glances at me, and I look down. Oops! There's half a cookie under the desk. I wonder if I can grab it while they aren't watching. I'm sorry I belittled her dead friend, but a cookie is a cookie. One has to have priorities. I sniff it. White chocolate and raisins, my favorite. I sneak closer.

"I decided I can't do this. I've tried so hard and suffered so much. I decided to return her and move on."

"I'd lie if I said I'm not disappointed. But it's your life and your choice."

I sneak and grab the cookie. It's yummy. Is there another? Nope. This is it. I lay my nose on my paws, trying to figure out how to whip Whippy into shape. I hope Silver finds a way to deal with her guilt.

"But then I changed my mind. I'll take her."

Take her? Take her where?

"So you commit to training her and handling her for her career?"

"I do."

"Why?"

"I thought you wanted me to do it."

"Sure. But why?"

"I'm not sure. Because she can read my thoughts and she was there when I needed her? Because it's time to move on? Because she always speaks her mind? I don't know. Either way, I'll take her."

"Good. Guinness, your explosives training starts tomorrow."

14

We stopped at PetSmart on the way home. I was delighted. I love shopping, especially for food. I looked for fried chicken. They didn't have it. Blue cheese, maybe? Nope.

This wasn't all that it was cracked up to be. I left Silver struggling to decide on a bed, a shedding brush, and a backpack, and I went in the back to check out the spa. Mud bath, anyone? Nope. Just a standard poodle with a freshly shaved beak having her hair dried. Her white barrel chest and the pom-poms on her hips made her look like a giant popcorn kernel. I choked with laughter. She glared at me.

"I beg your pardon?"

"Sorry. Just something I remembered."

I took off, acting like I was looking to adopt one of the cats in the aquarium. I pretended I didn't hear the poodle's snide comments to a Pekinese having his nails done.

"German shepherd, of course. How pedestrian. She wouldn't know chic if it hit her in the muzzle."

The Pekinese yapped something, but I don't speak Chinese. Moreover, the orange cat started hissing, and her compatriots followed. Wouldn't it be fun to get one for Silver, I thought? And I could chase it, too. I tried to squeeze back through the employee door when Silver clipped her leash to my collar.

"What are you doing here? I thought I lost you."

I smiled and bared my teeth to the orange. He hissed like a defective hairdryer.

"Just making new friends. You?"

Silver shook her head.

"Let's get you some food."

Great idea, I thought. But then I saw they had nothing there but kibble. No chicken, no bacon, not even popcorn. Nothing but kibble. Like, seriously?

"You like chicken or lamb?"

"Chicken? Where?"

She pointed to a bag of kibble. No, thanks.

"I prefer popcorn. Or a sandwich."

"You can't live on popcorn and sandwiches."

"Try me."

She bought a forty-pound bag of kibble with the picture of a Malinois on it. I smirked.

"Now, now, Guinness. Get over it. It just happens to be the large breed food with joint protection. It's not my fault they put the picture of a Malinois on it."

True that. But that's how advertising works. They make you think they'll give you happiness, but they sell you what they have. Like those stupid dogs, crazy about tick protection. Or the smiling humans sweating on their bikes. That's how they snag you. Even I fell for it. I wanted to make Shorty happy, so I tried to get him a blue pill, but I couldn't find his credit card.

We get home. Silver lays my bed in the bedroom and opens a Labatt's.

"Yes, please."

"That's not good for you," she says, pouring a little in my bowl. "Who taught you to drink beer?"

"Shorty. But he drank Bud Light."

She takes something out of the freezer and pops it in the microwave, then pours a cup of the new kibble in my bowl.

"There."

I sniff it from far away.

"Why don't I wait until your stuff is ready. Tell me, what changed your mind?"

She shrugs.

"I'm not a cat person. And the nursery's nothing but a pipe dream. I don't have a green thumb. I even hate mowing the grass."

I check her thumbs. Sure enough, they're both brown.

"So?"

"There aren't many things I'm good at. I don't garden; I don't cook; I'm not good with people. But I'm good with dogs. I can hear their thoughts."

"And?"

"I thought about what you said in the waiting room. You're right. Bear was the center of his universe, not me. It just dawned on me that he didn't die to save my life. He died for his neurosis. Anyhow, here we are."

The microwave beeps, and she takes out something smelling worse than dog food.

"What is it?"

"Beef Merlot with broccoli."

"Are you sure? Did you sniff it?"

"Well, you're the sniffing specialist around here. You tell me."

I sniff again. There may be a little beef and even some dead broccoli, but I can't recognize a dozen other things. You see, we dogs smell things differently than humans. Humans smell the composite and come up with a label. Like when you walk into Grandma's house for Christmas and the scent bowls you down, you think apple pie. I smell apples, cinnamon, butter, sugar, and nutmeg. I put them together, and I think apple pie. But the things in her meal? I don't know what they are, but I don't believe they're food.

"Read the label."

"Water. Onions. Modified corn starch. Beef flavor. Seasoned cooked beef and binder product. Maltodextrin. Potassium chloride. Potassium phosphate."

She throws the plate in the trash, then takes another sip of Labatt's.

"How about popcorn? Or you can have my kibble."

That evening, we lie on the sofa as she scratches my ears and tells me about the job.

"You won't have any trouble sniffing; you're a natural. The hard part is knowing when to signal me. They'll present you with all sorts of odors. Some matter, some don't. You'll have to learn those that have anything to do with explosives and point them out to me."

"How?"

"You sit by it. You don't paw at it, you don't rip it apart, and you don't bite it."

"Why not?"

She scratches her head with her front paw. How odd! I always use my hind paws or my teeth.

"Guinness, do you know what a bomb is?"

"I do. I watched war movies with Jones. It's something that blows up to destroy everything around it."

"Precisely. That's why you don't touch the bomb. You point it out to me, and I call the specialist who deactivates it. Your job is to find it, theirs to get rid of it."

"What if I miss it?"

"You won't. That's why we'll train. You won't miss it once you know what you're looking for."

I hope she's right. But how will I know what to look for if I've never seen it?

"Relax, Guinness. That's what training is all about. You'll be a shining star, I know it."

I take in a deep breath and mumble to myself: Don't let the bastages get you down.

"What?"

"That's what Jones said when things weren't going well. Except he didn't say 'bastages.'"

"He was a wise man."

"He still is. I surely hope he's not dead. If he died, who'll take care of Mom?"

"How long since you saw them, Guinness?"

"I last saw them in summer, when Shorty took me. I was a few months old."

"Not too long then. You know what?"

"No."

"If we make it through the training, we'll go visit them before we get deployed."

"Deployed?"

"Yes. That's when the Army sends us somewhere to look for mines and protect our soldiers."

"Where?"

"The Middle East, probably. Iraq or Afghanistan."

"Have you been there? How is it?"

"Different. The good news is that it's warm. And we'll be together with our brothers in arms."

"What's the bad news?'

"The bad news is that the enemy wants to kill us. And they often succeed."

15

The next day we started explosive detection. I was so busy that I forgot about Iraq, Afghanistan, and enemies.

We came to this massive hangar with a gleaming white floor covered by rows of metal cans. There's nothing but cans, six feet apart, as far as the eye can see. And two other K-9 teams. Two rows ahead of us, a yellow Lab drags a tall black man on his leash. Further along, a sable Malinois glares at me down his nose then moves on, pulling a blonde woman in his wake. Yikes! I'm getting tired of these freaking Malinois.

They've clearly been here before. The K-9s swiftly sniff their way from one can to the other, dragging their handlers behind. What the heck, I can do that with the best of them, I think, and I launch in hot pursuit, but Silver holds me back.

"Not so fast, Sparky. You first need to learn what to look for."

She takes me to a line of cans standing by the wall at the far side of the building.

"Check these out. These are the smells you need to find."

I sniff the first one. Acrid and chemical. Totally unattractive. I move to the next. This one is even acrider but less chemical. So is the following. And the next.

I'd be lying if I said they smell like crap. Crap smells good. But this? Nah. Not a single one in the lot is worth finding if you ask me. I wouldn't roll in any of them if you paid me in popcorn. But maybe for bacon...Oh well. If that's what Silver wants me to find, I'll find it.

We start on the grid, looking for the awful odors that Silver had me learn. I sniff gently, wary of having my delicate nose scorched by those miserable fumes.

Mamma Mia! This is heaven! The first one's manure. Then cat litter. Then bacon!

I paw at the can of bacon, struggling to open it. Silver freezes.

"Guinness! What are you doing? You're supposed to sit!"

"Relax, it's not a bomb. It's bacon! I'm trying to get it. Don't you want some?"

Silver sighs.

"There's no bacon in there, Guinness. Just the smell of it."

"How do you get the smell without the bacon?"

"Well, there is a little bacon, but not much. And it's not there for you to eat."

"Then what is it there for?"

"It's there to do exactly what it did. Distract you from your work. We waste our time talking about bacon when you have a hundred cans to check and find what we talked about: dynamite, TNT, water gel, RDX, urea nitrate, and hydrogen peroxide."

My bad. I hang my head and flatten my ears. I was not a good dog.

I start again along the row of cans, smelling each one and trying to ignore the fascinating smells. Rose Dove! I love rose soap, even though it gives me diarrhea. Mowed grass. Dead fish, aged. Heavenly!

I reluctantly move on.

Oops! Someone peed here. It's got to be the yellow lab.

I glance to see what he does. He's clearly ahead in his training, and I can use all the help I can get. He sniffs, then sits by a can a few rows down. His handler pets him and gives him a snack.

I stare at Silver.

"How about a snack?"

"As soon as you find what we're looking for."

I try to memorize the can the lab sat by, but they all look the same. I move on. Pepperoni. Gasoline. Olive oil.

Oops! This one's different. It smells like garlic, but it's not. It's faint, but sharp and persistent. It lingers, scratching the inside of my nostrils. I sit.

"Good girl, Guinness. Nice job," Silver says, offering me a snack. I smell it. It's kibble.

"Seriously? After all this work? I can get that at home."

"No longer, baby. No more free food for you. From now on, you'll have to work for your food, just like everyone else."

"How about some popcorn, at least?"

"Not here. We have to go by the book."

"Tonight?"

Silver hides her smile. I take the kibble and move to the next can, then the next.

That evening we eat popcorn and watch *Babe*, the shepherd pig. Silver thought it would motivate me with my training.

"He's got a heck of a way with sheep," I say, as he parlays his flock into reorganizing.

"He's a pig, not a shepherd. Unlike you, he doesn't have shepherding in his DNA. But he's doing a good job. He uses his strengths to overcome his weaknesses."

"I guess I'm envious. I'd rather work with sheep than with cans. They're more fun. They escape, and you get to run after them. You can run after them even if they don't escape. And you're outside."

"Me too. But remember, this is just the beginning of your training. As soon as we're done with the cans, we'll go outside."

"When?"

"After you learn all the smells. You've got to be 100 percent accurate."

"What's that?"

"When you find every explosive, no matter how strong or how faint the smell is, and you never make mistakes."

"When will that be?"

"In a few weeks, hopefully."

"And afterward?"

"We'll get our assignment and go to real work."

"Where?"

"Wherever they send us. In an airport, checking people's luggage, with a police department, or with the military. Wherever they need us the most. The demand for explosive detection K-9s went through the roof after 9/11. There's never enough of them, even though we import oodles from Europe. You'll be in big demand, Guinness."

"I don't want to be in big demand."

"What do you want, then?"

"I want to have fun. Learn things. Go places."

"We'll do that too. I got an idea. If you are as good as I think you will be, we'll go compete in NORT."

"What's NORT?"

"The National Odor Recognition Test. That's like the Olympics of explosive detecting K-9s. The best K-9s in the country and their handlers compete to recognize odors, perform searches, and find firearms and ammunition. We'll also learn the newest trends in homemade explosives."

Compete? That's me, all right. I'll get to show them who's boss.

"Will there be any Malinois at NORT?"

"Probably."

"Let's go then!"

16

I didn't really expect to win NORT. Neither did Silver, I'm sure. She just wanted to challenge me to get better while I tried to show her that a German shepherd is better than a Malinois any day of the week.

It turns out that NORT wasn't just for German shepherds and Malinois. At NORT, K-9s came in all sizes, colors, and shapes: Labradors, Dutch shepherds, golden retrievers. There were even some pathetic creatures that didn't look like dogs. I was just about to pounce after some sort of misshapen cat with crooked legs and a dogged attitude when Silver pulled me back.

"Stop that, Guinness. You'll get us disqualified. You're not supposed to attack your competitors."

"Competitors? Are you serious? That thing over there is competing in NORT?"

"Don't be racist, Guinness. This is not the Westminster Dog Show. Here, breed doesn't matter. What matters is how good you are. So what if he's a mixed breed? His focus and his nose may be better than yours. What will you think if he wins?"

If he wins? What will I think if he wins? I will be humiliated forever. I'll never be able to hold my tail up again. Lose to that?

I snapped to attention and followed Silver's commands like I meant business. I didn't even glance at the evil little thing when he passed by and growled at me as if he were a real dog. Phew! What an abomination! I was bigger than that when I was twelve weeks old. Prettier, too, I bet. I never had a pig snout and a thin, bald tail like a giant rat. I told him all that, by the way. I held my head up and waved my tail in dismissal, without ever looking his way. When he started yapping like a maniac, I pretended I had nothing to do with it. His poor handler didn't know what hit him, but Silver gave me the "I know you're up to something" look. She suspected it was me, but she couldn't be sure. Humans, even the smart ones, don't get these signals. How could they? They have no tails, and they can't even move their ears. It's a wonder they can communicate at all. Either way, that mutt was gone before the finals while I qualified. Silver was ecstatic.

"Good job, Guinness. Few dogs ever get a NORT Finalist certificate."

That didn't impress me one bit, since I can't read. I don't even have a wall to hang it on. But I was happy for Silver. That meant a lot to her. Personally, I'd rather have a bone. Maybe coming?

"What will they give us if we win? A cake? A bone? A hamburger, at least?"

"The first three get medals. The winner gets a trophy."

"A trophy?"

"Yep. Like a cup."

"A cup of what?"

"Just a cup. With ribbons and such."

Ribbons? Are you serious? And a cup? I don't need a cup. I have two bowls, one for water and one for food, and they work just fine. Humans are silly, I tell you. What's the point of giving a certificate to someone who can't read, a medal to someone who already has a tag on their collar, or an empty cup to someone who has two bowls? And it's not just me. I'll bet you two bones against a rolled newspaper that the other K-9s can't read either.

Oh well. I wasn't competing for the cup, anyhow. I was competing for bragging rights and for Silver. So, I forgot about the stupid cup and pushed on.

There were six of us left in the finals. Me, a chocolate Lab, another German shepherd, and three Malinois. Three of them! Overachievers!

The first test was to take our handlers through the field of smelly cans, identify the explosives and sit by them to signal our handlers.

As we sit in a windowless room with the other teams waiting for our turn, I smell Silver's stress sweat as she eyeballs the Malinois.

"Guinness, don't forget that accuracy trumps speed," she whispers.

I lick her hand to make her feel better.

"Relax."

"There are sixty cans with twenty odors, and you have to find every single one of them!"

"Roger that."

She pets me, but her hands are cold and clammy. Fortunately, we don't have long to wait. They call us, the door opens, and we're in the field of metal cans.

"Now's your time, Guinness."

I feel her heart pumping at the end of her leash as I pull her from can to can. Detergent. Ancho chiles. Gasoline. Cloves. Turpentine. Hickory. Garlic.

I sit next to the can of TNT.

Silver raises her hand to signal, and the referee nods.

"Go, Guinness."

I burst ahead, pulling Silver with me. Latex. Alcohol. Lard. Iodine. Coffee.

I sit next to the fertilizer. Silver raises her hand. The referee nods.

"Go, Guinness."

Milk. Lanoline. Onions. Cinnamon. I sit next to the hydrogen peroxide. Silver raises her hand. The referee nods.

Lemongrass. Acrylics. Bacon.

I ignore it and push forward.

Popcorn.

Like really?

I sit next to the gunpowder, which is the last can in the field. Silver raises her hand, the referee nods, and just like that, we're out, and Silver hugs me with tears in her eyes.

"We won?"

"Not yet, but you did a fantastic job. I'm so proud of you!"

I resist the urge to pull away. I'm not much into PDA, to be honest, but I don't want to hurt her feelings. I clear my throat.

"Is there some bacon in my future?"

"As soon as we get home."

We wait until they call the results. The Lab's out. So is the other German shepherd and one of the Malinois.

There are three of us left for the final phase. No matter what, Silver will get a medal, and she's happy beyond belief.

I'm happy too. Not for the medal. For the bacon.

And I'm looking forward to showing those Malinois what's what.

17

I woke up and remembered it was the day of the NORT finale. I did an upward dog, then a downward dog, then I shook. I was ready.

I came to the kitchen looking for breakfast.

"You slept like a log," Silver says, pouring milk over my Cheerios.

"Sugar?"

"It's not good for you." She adds a spoonful of sugar, and I inhale my breakfast, wondering about sleeping logs. I've never seen one wake up, not even when I peed on them. I thought they were dead. It turns out they're just asleep. Go figure.

"How about you?" I ask, cleaning up the milk I spilled on the floor.

"I'm fine."

I don't think so. Silver's tidy as usual, with her tight bun and her clean uniform, but her tired red eyes and her crumpled face show me she didn't get any sleep.

"What's wrong, girl? We did OK! I even got you a medal!"

"You did great. But that was yesterday. Today's the real deal. We'll have a mission search, a box search, a vehicle search, and then the field search. The cans were easy. This is going to be tricky.

You'll have to look into every nook and cranny, and you won't even know what you're looking for."

"Piece of cake, baby. If those stinky Malinois can do it, I can too. Just watch me."

Silver shakes her head. That's what people do. If she were a dog, she'd shake all over, like Mom, to show me that I'm full of it.

"I'm glad you're feeling confident, Guinness, but too much confidence is dangerous. This is all about paying attention and being thorough. Being cocky may trip you up. A little paranoia will take you further."

"What's paranoia?"

"It's when you think that everybody's out to get you."

Are you kidding? I don't think they are; I know they are. My paranoia's just fine, thank you.

The Malinois and I take turns through the searches. I find some fertilizer in a box, a couple of spent cartridges in the hangar, and a suspicious device that turns out to be an IED inside the car's tire. All that's left is the field search. We all load into a truck—the Malinois, their handlers, Silver, and me—and we get moving.

The truck drops from pothole to pothole, creaking like it's about to fall apart. I sit between Silver's legs, grabbing on to the floor, and study my two opponents. The one on the left is slate gray with sharp dark ears and fierce eyes. He'd be handsome if he weren't a Malinois. Well, maybe he's handsome anyhow.

He eyeballs me and slaps his tail on the floor.

"Hello, baby. How's it going?"

"Fine, thanks. And you?"

"Frank, are you fraternizing with the enemy or just trying to distract her?" asks the one on the right. He's almost black but for his pink tongue hanging sideways to his knees.

"Shut up, Jesse. She's not the enemy; she's just the competition. We may as well be civil. What's your name, beautiful?"

"Guinness. Guinness Van Jones."

"Are you Dutch?" Jesse asks.

"Of course not. I'm a German shepherd." I lift my chin to show off the elegant line of my long black muzzle. "You boys Belgian, I presume. Are you related?"

"Yep. Jesse's my littermate. We enrolled together. We're a military family. Father was a Marine."

"So was mine."

"Don't say! Hey, what are you doing tonight?"

Who knows? Eating bacon, I hope, but I don't have to answer since the truck stops.

"The first team out!"

"See you guys later." Jesse pulls his handler to the field.

We sit and wait. The tension is thick enough to bite through when Jesse returns and mumbles something in Belgian to his brother.

Frank's next. He drags his handler out, and we wait again. Jesse lays his muzzle on his feet, pretending to sleep.

"How was it?" I ask.

He opens one yellow eye.

"Lousy. There's a whole field out there full of crap you need to search. You'd better have a system; otherwise, you'll lose track."

He's right. I jump out of the truck in a fenced grass field full of things. Piles of tires. Debris. A shed. Scattered barrels. A mountain of boxes. A bunch of trees and bushes.

"Crap," Silver mumbles. I'm not sure if it's a command, but it sounds like a good idea.

"Search!"

System, he said. I'll show you system.

I start left and sniff everything to the fence, then turn around and come back to the other wall, stopping by to check everything on my way. I smell the tires, crawl under a bush, sniff the boxes. I sit.

Silver raises her hand, and the observer nods. She finds the gun hidden inside a box and takes it.

"Search."

I sniff around the shed, then go inside and sniff the toolbox. I get out again, and I smell the fence as I get to it, then turn around again, in a grid pattern. I sit by the pine tree.

Silver signals.

The observer nods. Silver picks up the ammunition hidden in the branches, and we move on forward, always in a tight grid pattern. We find a bag of fertilizer in a box, a box of ammunition inside a truck tire, then a grenade under a rusty wheelbarrow.

I'm done, but to be extra-sure, I scan the field again, in the opposite direction this time. That's it.

I sit and look at Silver.

"Are you sure?"

I slap my tail to the ground. Silver calls it.

"We're done, sir."

"Congratulations."

The boys don't speak to me on the way back. They pretend to be asleep, but I know better.

The bacon was delicious, crisp, flavorful, and crunchy. Silver sat on the sofa holding the cup and watched me eat as my medal clanged against my bowl.

"Have some," I said. "It's better than that empty cup! Or at least pour a beer in it!"

"I'm so proud of you, Guinness. Is there anything else you'd like besides that bacon?"

I lick my bowl clean.

"Now that you mention it, there is one thing."

"What?"

"I'd like to visit Mom."

18

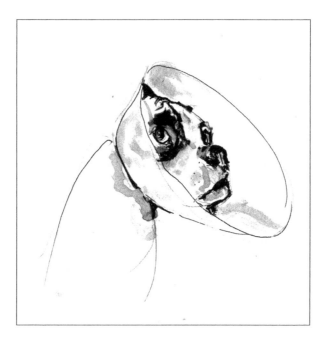

Winning NORT was the high point of my training. Even more so after Silver started drinking her coffee out of her cup. I felt like I got her something useful. Plus, we were on vacation.

We went out for long walks and watched movies with popcorn every evening. Life was good.

Until the day Silver had a long talk with the colonel, and she came out looking grim. We drove home in silence. I wondered what was up. She poured us a beer, then looked at me with teary eyes.

"Guinness, you know I love you."

My hackles went up. That was no good. Whatever was coming was awful news. I took a deep breath and steeled myself to get it.

"What is it? Something wrong with Mom? Are you about to die too? Have you changed your mind and decided to get a cat instead of me?"

Silver shook her head.

"Guinness, have you ever thought about having puppies?"

"Poppies? I'd rather have some bacon."

"Puppies. Like small dogs."

"I had puppies. My littermates: Yellow, Black, Green, Brown, White, and Purple. They were fun. I was Red."

"No. I mean having your own puppies."

"They were my own. My own brothers and sisters."

"Would you like to be a mom?"

I freeze.

"Are you kidding? I can't be Mom."

"Why not?"

"I'm not smart enough. And I don't have the patience. Mom's a genius. I'm nothing like her. If you're going to get me something, get me a cat. Chasing them is a good sport."

Silver sighs.

"Good then. The colonel told me you'll have to get spayed before we deploy."

"What's spayed?"

"Guinness, the Army is a full-time job. You've got to give it all you've got. They can't have working K-9s having puppies on the base. That's why you'll have surgery before we go, to make sure you don't have puppies."

"Is that like having a bath?"

I hate baths. I'd swim all day, and I'd roll in the mud forever, but a bath? No, thanks. It's not the water; it's the shampoo. I work hard every day to hold on to my good smells. Whenever I find something smelling sexy, I'll roll in it, whether it's dead fish, horse manure, or poop. But if they give you a bath, it's all over. You end up fluffy and smelling like perfume. Embarrassing! Don't get me wrong now, I love soap, especially Rose Dove, even though it gives me diarrhea. That's why I limit myself to half a bar.

Silver sighs.

"Not quite, but it's not much fun. But I'll have some bacon for you when you come through."

"Come through? Come through what?"

She takes me out, even though I don't need to go. I wonder if it's just to change the subject. But then we drive to the vet, and I forget. She hugs me and sniffs.

"You're going to be all right. This is the best vet this side of the Atlantic."

She's gone before I can ask anything else, and a girl in scrubs leads me to an exam room, giving a wide berth to a barking bulldog wearing a lampshade.

"What happened to you, Bully? They ran out of lamps?"

He sputters toward me, but his leash holds him back.

"Don't forget you're plugged in," I say, then they give me a shot, and I fall into a burst of colors. I'm twirling faster and faster inside a swirl of rainbows. I remember Shorty telling Whippy about his old dog crossing the rainbow bridge, and I wonder. Will I cross it too? If I don't return, who'll take care of Silver? She's my responsibility. I should have planned who to leave her to.

I wake up to Silver watching me. That, I like. What I don't like is the lampshade around my neck. What's with these people and their lamps?

"How are you, Guinness?"

I'm groggy, and my tongue is so dry I can barely mumble. But I don't want to worry Silver.

"Good. You?"

She pets my head, but she looks like she's far away.

"Does it hurt?"

"Sort of. But I'm mainly hungry. Did you say bacon?"

She shakes her head.

"One day, you're going to die from a heart attack. You need to learn to like vegetables. And fruit."

"I do."

"Which?"

"Grapes. Raisins. White chocolate."

When we get home, she cooks my bacon. It smokes and sizzles, and I slobber as the scent fills my nose.

"There. But that's just for tonight. Starting tomorrow, we'll eat healthily."

I ignore her words but I inhale the bacon, every little crumb of it. She fills my water bowl and sighs.

"You know, Guinness, I always wanted children. That's like puppies for humans."

"I know. I met one. It tasted great. It was covered in whipped cream. So what happened?"

"When I was sixteen, I had a boyfriend; I became pregnant. That's like expecting puppies."

"And?"

She looks away to hide the tears streaming down her cheeks. She sighs and hugs herself.

"I was too young. The baby died inside me, and he wouldn't come out. They had to take him out to save my life. I could never have kids after that."

Her sorrow is so raw that I can feel her suffering, even through my fogged brain.

"I'm sorry, Silver." I lick her face as best I can from inside that darn lamp shade, and I almost scoop out one eye, but she doesn't complain.

"To my people, being a woman was all about having kids. If I couldn't have kids, it was like I stopped being a woman. My boyfriend left me. Even my mom ignored me to focus on my sisters. That's how I got into dogs. Dogs didn't care whether I had kids. They loved me just as I was. So I joined the Army as a K-9 handler. That was my best decision ever. My second one was to take you."

I don't understand what she says, but I feel her pain. And I'm sorry.

But I'm fogged and tired. My belly is on fire like they ripped something out, and that darn lamp shade cuts me away from Silver and the world. I can't even lick the burn in my belly. So I lick her once more, then I lay down to rest. She sniffs.

"Thanks, Guinness. I hope this won't leave you hollow like it left me."

I'm sorry she hurts. My belly's on fire, but her pain is in her soul. That's got to hurt worse.

19

The days got shorter and the leaves started turning. Vacation was over, and it was time to go. I wasn't ready to get deployed, but I don't think anyone ever is. Not even Silver, though she knew what was coming.

She packed Bear's picture, my medal, her trophy, and some popcorn. She added some clothes for herself and my bulletproof vest. I have no other clothes, so I pack light, but I'm always dressed for the occasion.

The trip to Afghanistan was long and not much fun. After all the movies I'd seen, I couldn't wait to fly, but it turns out that I was cargo. I spent long hours locked in a crate with no view and no entertainment other than the engine noise. And the odors.

Odors being one of my areas of expertise, I started sniffing the cargo and making up stories about them to pass the time.

There were gasoline and oil and all the usual mechanical smells, but there were some fascinating scents here and there. The peppered pastrami and pickles to my left got me drooling like crazy and made my stomach growl. Somebody bringing home a gift of food, I thought. The golf bag next to me gave a faint whiff of cat pee. They must have locked the cat with the bag, and the cat made sure it won't happen again. From somewhere up in front, I sniffed a full set of essential oils: bergamot, chamomile, eucalyptus, lavender —the whole lot. One of those naturopaths hell-bent on curing cancer with tea-tree oil?

All of a sudden, I sniff a dog.

Really?

I sniff again. I'll be darned if that's not a Labrador, somewhere behind me.

"Hey! Buddy!"

Claws scratch the floor, then someone barks.

"Hey. Where are you?"

"A few bags ahead, I think. How's it going?"

"Awful! I need help!"

She sounds miserable. I am too, but I'm a German shepherd, so I can't show it. It would be beneath my dignity. I'd rather chew on my tail and struggle to hold my bladder than ask for help.

"What's your problem, buddy?"

"I've been locked in this cage for ages. I'm hungry, I'm thirsty, and I need to pee."

"Roger that. Same here. Who are you?"

"I'm Corporal Butter. I'm a K-9 en route to Afghanistan. You?"

"Name's Guinness. Guinness Van Jones. We'll get there, buddy. Just relax."

"I can't relax. I need to pee."

I swear silently and cross my legs.

"Me too. But it may take a while. How about peeing in a corner?"

"I can't pee in my crate! I've never done that, not even when I was a puppy!"

I've never done that either, but it ain't looking like any juniper bushes are coming my way soon. I sigh and squeeze into a corner to squat, but I change my mind. Boys raise their legs and pee sideways. What if I try it?

I focus on the cat-smelling golf bag, and lift my leg. That feels weird, with the plane moving under me and all. Oh well. I let go, and the golden stream flows out my crate and sprays the bag like it's a mailbox. Hah! There may be a few drops inside, but that's nothing. I'll call this a success.

"Hey, Butter?"

"Yes."

"Are you a girl?"

"Of course."

"Me too. Have you ever peed like a boy?"

"No."

"How about trying? I just did, and I feel so much better. And my cage is almost clean."

I hear shuffling, scratching, and movement, then running water; finally, a sigh of relief.

"Thanks, Guinness. This is much better. I'm still hungry and thirsty, but I'm better. I hate soiling myself."

"Is this your first deployment?"

"Nope. My third. You?"

"My first. What do you do?"

"I sniff explosives. No matter where you go in Afghanistan, tons of IEDs, Improvised Explosive Devices, are ready to explode. Even when they don't kill anyone, they prevent people from living their lives, working their fields, and sending their kids to school. After we clear them, they get to live a better life."

"You must feel so proud."

"Sometimes. But I mostly feel tired. My handler and I have done this so many times that it's getting old."

"You like your handler?"

"I love him. I love his wife and the kids even more. It was hard for us to leave our family and come back here. I hope to retire soon."

"What will you do when you retire?"

"Take long walks? Play with the kids? Chase cats? I don't know, but I can't wait to find out."

I lay in my crate with my nose on my paws, thinking about Silver. What will she do if she retires? She has no kids. No hobbies. She doesn't have anyone but me. And for some reason, that reminds me of Mom.

20

Silver kept her word. After NORT, we went to visit Mom. It was both wonderful and strange to see my old home, the yard, the trees, the leaves turning. It was like I'd never left.

Silver rang the doorbell. Mom warned us off, and her voice made me feel all warm and squishy inside, even though I knew she thought we were the mailman.

Jones opened the door wearing his old red sweater, the one with the elbow hole I ate when he forgot me in the library. He looked at Silver, then at me. His jaw dropped, and he broke into tears. I put my paws on his shoulders and licked them off before anyone could see them.

"Red!"

"Who?"

The door flung open, and Mom flew out. She was smaller than I remembered; her black muzzle had turned gray, and her amber eyes cloudy, but her lovely pink tongue licked my nose just like she used to.

"Mom!"

"Red! It is you!"

"Mom!"

We jumped, barked, and played together, rolling around in the yard like puppies. Jones wiped his eyes with his sleeve, then blew his nose. Silver pretended not to notice.

"Thank you for bringing her, Miss..."

"Sergeant Silver."

"Thank you for bringing her, Sergeant Silver. This means a lot to Maddie and me. Red was our last pup since we're both too old to carry on. How's she doing?"

"She's doing fantastic. She just won NORT, which is like the Olympics for explosives detecting canines. There."

Silver handed him a picture of me trying to eat the medal dangling around my neck. It's not my best picture, since I had to cross my eyes to see the medal, but she's very proud of it. She framed it and put it on the wall next to Bear's photo.

"I brought this for you. There she is, winning NORT."

Jones choked, and I didn't know if he was laughing or crying. Mom licked my face.

"I'm so proud of you, Red."

"I love you, Mom."

As we got ready to leave, Jones asked Silver, "Did you know she can sing?"

Silver looked at him like he'd lost it.

"Guinness?"

"Yep. Watch."

He fumbles with his phone, and just like that, the call of my people stirs my soul. Mom lifts her muzzle to the sky and starts singing. I can't help but follow, and Jones joins us.

"A time to be born, a time to die; a time to plant, a time to reap; A time to kill, a time to heal."

"A time to laugh, a time to weep," Silver sings along, wiping her eyes.

That was the last time I saw Mom.

Thinking of her makes me choke. I sigh and turn in my cage, trying to find a better spot, but, after all this time, I'm running out of spots.

"Guinness?"

"Yes, Butter."

"What are you going to do in Afghanistan?"

"Whatever they tell me, I guess."

"Are you an explosive sniffing dog? Will you go looking for land mines?

"I think so."

"We may work together."

"That would be nice. I could use a friend."

"Me too."

I wake up as they drag my crate through the door. I get a glimpse of a concrete floor and dark green walls before they store me with the rest of the luggage.

"Guinness?" Butter calls.

"Yes?"

"You OK?"

She sounds really close, so I peek through the holes of my crate, looking for her in the pile of luggage. I can't see her, but I can smell her, a soothing smell of Labrador. I love Labradors. They are the kindest, nicest, friendliest dogs in the world. Better than German shepherds, you ask? Well. We German shepherds don't think about ourselves as dogs. We're people.

"I'm hanging in there. You?"

"Me too. Hey Guinness?"

"Yes?"

"We girls ought to get together. Look me up when you land. I'm an explosive detecting canine. My handler's name is Brown. You?"

"I'm an MPC, multi-purpose K9. My handler's name is Silver. They also call her Bridge."

"Bridge? The Malinois's Bridge?"

"Maybe?"

"That dog blew himself up just to show everybody he was right. What an ice-hole. Bridge is lucky to be rid of him, even if she doesn't know it. She's a lovely girl. You'll be all right with her."

"Thanks, Butter. See you soon, I hope."

Somebody loads my crate on a trolley.

"Same here, girlfriend. Stay safe."

Minutes later, Silver comes to check on me.

"You OK, Guinness?"

"Splendid. You?"

"I'm sorry, Guinness. I know it was a long trip, but it's almost over. I'm glad to see you're all right."

Me too, I think, as they roll me somewhere like I'm luggage.

21

The first thing I notice about Afghanistan is the heat. I've never seen heat like this before, not even when people complained, sweated, and walked around in their underwear. All but me, of course. My coat is my uniform, swimsuit, and winter coat, all in one. I dress the same at –10 as I do here, at 105. I'm very proud of my shiny black coat, but right now, I'd trade it for something skimpy and sleeveless, even if it were ruffly and pink. But that's not an option, so I just lie in my crate, panting like a train engine.

After the heat, the next thing I can't miss is the dust covering everything: roads, cars, people. It's everywhere, like snow in winter, but it's not white and pretty. It's dull beige, like desert camo, and it doesn't melt. It's so light that I raise a cloud if I swig my tail, and so thick that I see nothing beyond twenty feet. Whenever I sniff, it gets into my nose, and I sneeze. And right then and there, I know the dust is my enemy.

I bare my teeth and bark at it, but it only gets thicker. I growl and try to bite it, but it's like biting air. I get nothing but a parched throat and a bad taste in my mouth.

"You'll get used to it," Silver says, as someone loads my crate in the back of a dusty truck. "You'll get so used to it you'll stop noticing it."

I don't think so. This nasty thing is so pervasive that I know I'll find it in my you-know-what when I get around to cleaning it.

Another crate gets loaded next to mine.

"Guinness! Is that you?"

"Butter?"

I sniff, trying to ignore the dust. Sure thing, it's Butter. I get to see her for the first time. She's light gold, the color of Irish butter, with silky ears and shiny brown eyes.

"I'm so glad we're together. Oh, my, aren't you good-looking," Butter says, eyeing me through the grid of her crate. "That elegant black muzzle with brown eyebrows and jowls. Nice markings."

"You're not so bad yourself."

I'm so embarrassed that I feel like blushing, but I don't know how. That's a Labrador for you. These Canadians would make you feel good even if your tail grew out of your forehead. We German shepherds have a more Teutonic approach.

"Nice coat," I say. "Ears too. When will they stand up?"

Butter laughs.

"Cut the crap, Guinness. I'm a Labrador. My ears don't stand up."

"Oh. I see. Well, they're pretty just the way they are."

"Thanks, kid. I'm so glad to be back on the ground. We're on the last stretch here. Just a couple more hours, and we should reach our base in Kandahar."

"I thought we were going to Afghanistan?"

"Of course. We are in Afghanistan. Kandahar is one of its provinces. The deadliest one. More American soldiers—K-9 and humans—died here than anywhere else in this country. Helmand comes next."

"Hell-man?"

"Helmand. Another province. I hope we get deployed together. Wouldn't that be great?

"I'd love that."

She falls asleep, but I can't. I stare through the grid of my crate, but there isn't much to see. We drive through miles and miles of dusty, empty roads between dusty, empty fields, leaving behind a cloud of dust. It's hot too, but the truck's open, so the heat's not bad. But, as far as the eye can see, there's nothing but scorched earth and dust. Every now and then, a tiny village with dust-colored mud houses, then more dust and desolation.

"I hate dust."

Butter opens her left eye.

"We all do, Guinness. But, against the dust, there's no winning. You can't fight it, you can't kill it, you can't ignore it. You need to accept it."

Every cell in my body wants to fight it, but I lay in wait, pretending to agree. Butter falls asleep again. We carry on through miles and miles of dust until the truck stops in front of a green metal gate topped with spikes. That's the only break in the ten-foot-tall mud wall, covered with rolls of evil-looking razor wire that seems to go on forever. The gate opens to let us in, then slams shut behind us, and my heart jumps. I hate being locked in.

Butter sighs with relief.

"We're safe now."

"Safe from what?"

"Guinness, we're inside the wire. This is our home, the one place we're safe since everything and everyone gets checked when they come in. Outside the wire, there's a big bad world. You never know where the strike will come from. Everybody there hates us. The roads and the fields are full of IEDs waiting to blow us up. The villages shelter snipers who are looking to kill us. Anyone there, from old men to kids, may throw a grenade or blow themselves up to kill us. There is no safety outside the wire."

I can see she means it. She speaks from a place of conviction, but I'm not so sure. I don't know if she's right, and everyone out there is trying to get us, or if she's paranoid. No wonder, after three deployments. But I don't want to hurt her feelings, so I keep my mouth shut.

"See, Guinness, that's why we're here. People can't smell worth a damn unless it's apple pie or hot pizza and wings. Bombs? Not so much. That's why they need us, K-9s, to find the IEDs and point them out to our handlers as they taught us in training. But this is not training; this is real. Every mistake could mean death—ours, or our people's. We scour the fields, the roads, and the villages for mines. Firearms, explosives, and ammo too. We track the bad guys and help our soldiers put them away. We're here to protect our soldiers, and we're essential. That's why the enemy wants us dead. They want us so bad that, if they had a choice, they'd rather kill one of us than a soldier. You've got to be paranoid to stay alive."

My hackles stand, and I don't know if I'm scared or angry, but I don't have time to wonder. My crate opens.

"Guinness, come."

I jump out and face-plant. My legs got numb from being locked in the cage. It's time for a little yoga. I raise my muzzle in an upward dog, then my rear in a downward dog, then I shake. That's not technically yoga, but it sets my blood pumping and helps rearrange my fur. That's my morning routine.

Butter's out too. We smell each other's butts, then she licks my nose, and I wag my tail. We're buddies now. I invite her for a playfight when I hear a growl behind me.

"Wow! Two new chicks! Welcome, girls. Good to see you."

I turn around to stare into the brown eyes of the largest Malinois I've ever seen. He smiles from one dark, sharp ear to the other as his brown tail beats frenetically, agitating the dust.

"Viper! You're still here?"

"Butter! It's you! You're back! Good to see you, partner. Your tail looks younger than ever. Who's the new chick?"

"This is Guinness. Guinness, meet Viper. He and I worked together before."

Her voice is so bland that I know there's more to it than meets the eye. I glance at the Malinois. He looks friendly enough, but I know better. These Malinois, they're all a bunch of neurotics.

"Hello, Guinness. Welcome to Kandahar. Glad to have you. How do you like it here?"

I raise my nose, take a deep breath, and I sneeze.

"I'd like it better if you'd stop raising the dust with your tail."

His smile fades. Butter stares at me.

"Like really? What bug have you got up your butt? I was just trying to welcome you."

"Thanks. But no, thanks."

I lift my tail up high and go visit Silver, who's shaking hands with a bunch of uniforms. She pets me.

"So good to see that you've made friends already. We're all a band of brothers here. We can't survive unless we have each other's back."

I glance back at Viper, who stares at me like I've grown a second tail. Crap.

Good job, Guinness. You started your deployment with a bang.

22

It turns out that fighting a war is far less exciting than watching it in the movies. On a scale of bacon to kibble, it's behind taking a bath and ahead of getting my nails clipped. Every day is the same. We sleep in our crates, then we wake up to watch our handlers cooking breakfast. They squeeze some lumpy paste out of a bag, mix it into kibble, and add hot water to get a snotty, smelly slop.

"There's your stew," Silver says, placing it in front of me.

Stew! I wish. I glare at her, then sniff the dish as if it were an IED. I pick a piece or two, then sit and watch it cool.

"That's good for you. It has vitamins and minerals and supplements for strong tendons and joints."

"Yeah, yeah, yeah."

Next to me, Butter inhales her food.

"Lamb! I love lamb."

Butter is passionate about food. Whether it's lamb, chicken, or parsnip, Butter gulps it with abandon and looks for more.

"The heck lamb. That's mutton. You can smell it all the way from Helmand, for God's sake," Viper says, picking at his food after carefully studying every single bit. The Malligator's not a foodie, I recon, from his lack of enthusiasm and his lean muscles. Unlike

Butter, he's one of those K-9s who gets his reward from the ball, like me.

It's not that I don't like food. I love food—the right food. I crave popcorn, bacon, and cookies, but there's none of that here. Nothing but MREs, Meals Ready to Eat, for all the soldiers, with or without tails. Every once in a while, Silver slips me her cheese crackers, but they aren't bacon. Not even popcorn.

After breakfast, we take our handlers for a walk. We keep them on a leash, of course. That's when we do our business, as best we can, since there are no juniper bushes, no trees, not even mailboxes. Nothing but cracked earth and dust. Oh, how I miss the green, green grass of home.

Then we train. We run, jump, fight, and apprehend fake suspects. Most importantly, we search for IEDs inside the wire: under the trucks, inside the supply sheds, along the roads.

Whenever we get it right, we get rewarded. Butter, like all Labradors, loves food. Give her a little kibble, and she'll work forever. Not me, baby! I'd work my heart out for a burger. Even a hot dog, but there's none here, so I have to settle for the ball. Whenever I find the stuff she planted, Silver throws me the ball, and I squeeze and chew on it like it's a Malinois. When I do an outstanding job, she gives it a few tugs, so I feel like I'm fighting prey. That's way better than kibble.

Viper, who's a Malinois and therefore inferior, prefers the ball too. That irks me, but not enough to give up mine, so we keep tabs on who gets the ball more often. We pretend not to, but we watch each other closely. I hate to say it, but he's sharp.

Day after day after day, we look for IEDs inside the wire. They're fake, of course; everything here gets triple-checked before coming in. It's also way too easy. I can see the dust disturbance and sniff Silver's scent before detecting the IED, even though she wears gloves. Still, it eases the boredom.

After training, we chill in our crates until the evening walk. Butter mostly sleeps, but I have too much time on my paws, and chilling's not my bowl of kibble, so I spend my time remembering the days I clammed with Shorty and sang with Mom and Jones. Then I get so sad that I have to get moving, so I get up and chase my tail for a quick pick-me-up, but I wake up Butter.

"I'm sorry, Butter. I just couldn't be still anymore."

"No worries, Guinness. I know you're restless. We'll go outside soon."

"Outside where?"

"Outside the wire. We'll go looking for real IEDs and real perpetrators, and you'll get more excitement than you bargained for. Whenever we go out, we never know who comes back."

She falls asleep again. I sigh, and I lay my nose on my paws. I hope she's right 'cause I'm not loving it here. This is not like home. There, we spent all our time together. Not here. Gone are our movies and popcorn. Silver spends her evenings chatting, laughing, and playing cards with the other soldiers. She still feeds me and trains me, but she often has better things to do. I'm glad she's happy and content; I just wish something would happen someday.

Then it does.

The gunfire starts as we're having breakfast.

"What the heck's that?" Viper asks.

"Some diversion somewhere," Butter mumbles between bites of food. "They can't be serious. Before breakfast? It's way too early to fight."

The alarm goes off—like anyone needs it, really, on top of all that ruckus. The soldiers squeeze into their bulky bulletproof vests, slap on their helmets, and run to answer the gunfire. Well, they don't exactly run since their kit's so heavy it slows them to a crawl. Still, they rush to the camouflage net to shoot, even though there's no way they can see anything beyond ten feet—the dust around the camp is thicker than a mud wall.

We K-9s finish our breakfast as the gunfire keeps on, hurting our ears. We're behind the wire, so there's no immediate threat. I wonder if we'll train this morning, when the lieutenant calls off the fire. His mouth is tight, and his eyes red with dust stay glued to the surveillance blimp floating in the pale sky above us.

"This was a diversion. Our aerial surveillance shows three insurgents planting IEDs along the road while their friends kept us under fire to distract us. They've mined the roads again. K-9s!"

The handlers line up.

"We'll sweep the roads, the neighboring fields, and the villages. Silver?"

"Yes, sir."

"You and Guinness go first. Your K-9 is brand new, and she needs the experience. Go."

"Yes, sir."

Silver's face is gray and tight as she buckles my vest, then attaches her thirty-foot leash to my collar. I know she's thinking about the last time she was on a mission. That's when she lost her Malinois. I wish I could say something to give her confidence, but I can't. So I just head toward the gate, and she follows. The others line up behind us at a safe distance.

"Guinness?"

"Yes."

"This is not about being fast; it's about being smart. This is not a competition. Take your time and make sure every darn inch of that road is safe. Go slow. If you do well, I'll make it worth it to you."

"Like how?"

"What do you want?"

"Popcorn and a movie."

"I'll get your popcorn and your darn movie if we come back alive. Now go."

23

The metal gate creaks open to the desolate desert outside the wire. There is no living thing as far as the eye can see—just the never-ending dusty road cutting through the dusty fields and the village compound down the road. Everything is dusty, silent, and empty. There's no one here but me, dragging Silver behind me on her leash. The others are way behind, keeping a safe distance, in case I step on the mine instead of sitting next to it like I'm supposed to.

"You can find it, Guinness."

I sure can. I just hope I find it before it finds me. I step out gingerly, sniffing the air while trying to keep out the dust, and I'm not winning.

"Good luck, Guinness."

That's Butter's bark, somewhere behind. I'll thank her later. But for now, I step carefully through the soft beige dust, sniffing every small step. I've never moved this slowly, but slow is smooth, and smooth is fast, Silver says.

As empty as this desert is, it's full of smells. Gasoline. Smoke. Sweat. Fear. Where can they be coming from, since there's not a living soul for miles?

I feel Silver's heartbeat at the other end of the leash. Butter was right when she said that here in Afghanistan, feelings go up and down the leash. Silver follows every step I take, and that gives me confidence. She trusts me enough to go wherever I take her. That makes me trust myself more.

I take another step, then another. Oops! An acrid, sharp odor overcomes the dust that caked my nose. That's explosive; I'd bet my life on it. Actually, I am. But where is it? I step softly as the toxic odor burns my nose. I sniff again, trying to ignore the dust. Fat chance!

Butter was right. Accept the dust. I stop fighting it, even though the idea of breathing it in makes me sick to my stomach. I zero in on the scent. It's to my right, just feet away. I fill my nose with it—and dust, of course. I step to where the ugly sharp odor fills my nose, right by the camp back gate.

I sit, pointing to the scent.

"We have a signal."

Silver follows my tracks, kneels beside me, then leans over to brush away the dust with feather-light fingers. The silence is deafening. Rivulets of sweat pour down her brown face into her eyes, then down her chin, dripping to cake the dust, but she barely blinks. She gently sweeps the dust away until suddenly, her sweat changes odor. Before, it was heat and stress. Now it's fear.

She clears her throat.

"I feel the pressure plate. That's a positive ID. Good job, Guinness." She retraces her steps. I follow. Seconds later, we're both back.

"Destroy," the lieutenant says.

Gunfire rips the silence. A moment later, the IED blows up in an angry pyre of flames twisting around each other like a nest of angry snakes hissing at the sky. The smell of smoke and destruction scorches my nose and fills my lungs. There's nothing left of the place we were at just seconds ago. I'd be there, burning, if I stepped on the darn thing.

"Good work, Guinness."

Silver's voice cracks. I pretend I don't notice. It's the first time I really understand how she must have felt when Bear blew up, and I'm so sorry.

We file back inside the wire, where there's no bomb other than those planted by the handlers. Butter was right; this is our only safe place. For the first time, inside the wire feels like home.

"Not too bad for a first-timer."

Viper looks at me down his long black snout, wagging his tail in approval.

"Shut up, Viper. She did great. Awesome work, girl," Butter says, congratulating me with a nose lick. "I couldn't have done better myself."

24

That first mission was the end of the beginning. I was no longer a rookie; I was a real K-9. After that, the base felt like a home rather than a prison. Seeing the dangers lurking outside the wire made me appreciate the safety of being inside. I even learned to accept the dust. Its softness protected my paws, and I could detect the slightest movement for miles since a moving mouse would lift a plume of dust.

My brothers-in-arms, both K-9 and humans, looked at me with newfound respect. Silver was so proud of me she could burst. It was almost like she forgot her Malinois, though I knew better. But she had come into her own.

"See, Guinness, NORT was special. I'll never forget the joy of seeing you win. But competition is just that: a competition. This stuff here is real. Real life, real death. This is where you learn who to trust. I always knew I could trust you, but now, every person on the base feels safer when you lead them outside the wire. You've got your baptism by fire."

I don't know what baptism is, but I know fire. Silver was right. The soldiers would stop to say "Hi" as they went about their day. They'd slip me a tasty bit of their MRE when they thought nobody was watching. Even Viper started offering me his butt to smell first every morning. Now that's respect!

That's another strange thing about humans: they don't sniff each other's butts. You'd wonder how they even recognize each other. For us K-9s, sniffing butts is more than a handshake. Sniffing each other's butt is a combo of passport check, checking each other's resume, and peeking at each other's calendar.

Whenever I sniff Viper's butt, I first check that he's still a boy. You never know when he'll change his mind. By sniffing his butt, I can tell if he's healthy or ill, what he ate, and if he's in a good mood. I also find out if he feels like dating. For those who don't know: the dominant dog always sniffs first. When Viper offers me his butt to smell, it's like he bows to me. And I'm humbled. Well, sort of. We German shepherds aren't much into humble.

Regardless, those were the days. We gulped our breakfast glop, made trails in the dust, then played hide-and-sick with explosives.

After dinner, we chilled telling stories—we K-9s, in our quarters, the bipeds in theirs.

One evening when Viper was sniffing somewhere else, Butter and I lay watching the soldiers play cards. She cleaned her tail real good, making it glow with the light, and it just struck me that Butter didn't look like a military dog. She was friendly and soft and kind, but there was nothing military about her. She loved food and never had a bad word for anyone—unlike Viper or me.

I had to ask.

"Butter, how did you get into the military?"

Her ears went down, and she glanced around to make sure nobody was listening.

"Guinness, can you keep a secret?"

"Of course."

"I'm... I'm not a purebred. I'm just a mutt, you see. My mother made a mistake, and she had an unexpected litter. Her owner couldn't sell us as purebreds, so he dropped us off at a dog shelter. That's where Brown found me when he came looking for a dog to train. So, here I am."

"What does being a mixed breed have to do with anything?"

"Oh, Guinness. There's your pure-bred privilege. Of course, you don't understand. People want purebreds, so they're worth a lot of money. That's why there are so many horrible puppy mills squeezing money and oppressing dogs. But nobody wants to pay for a mutt—unless they're one of those silly designer Labradoodles or Yorkipoos.

I struggle to understand, but I can't. I'm supposed to have a lengthy pedigree, but nobody wanted me either. I don't get it, but this isn't about me. This is about Butter.

"What mix are you?"

"That's the problem. I don't know. If I did, I could call myself a LabraPoo or a PitLab. I could do my best to look important. I could even pretend that's how I was meant to be and start a new fad. But I can't, so I just pretend I'm a Labrador and hope that nobody finds out."

"Oh, come on, get over it, Butter," Viper growls, dropping to the ground next to us. He's been on a long trip somewhere, and his tongue hangs to his knees from running in the heat.

Butter's eyes drop to the ground, and her tail hides between her legs. She's mortified.

"Leave her alone," I snarl.

Viper growls.

"Shut up, Guinness. Butter, nobody here cares about your breed. This isn't a pet store or a puppy mill; we're all K-9s here. I'm a Malinois, Guinness is a shepherd, you're a Labrador mix. None of that really matters. We're all in this together. It's the same with the soldiers: Silver's brown, Brown's black, and my handler, Sabrina, is Latina. So what? Nobody cares about your pedigree. The only thing people care about is how you do your job. And you're doing a fantastic job, Butter. I'm glad to work with you."

Butter sits up a little straighter.

"Thanks, Viper. That's kind of you."

I lick her nose.

"As he said."

"Thanks, guys. I'm so glad to have you as my brothers."

After that evening, I started looking differently at Viper. He wasn't just an ice-hole, after all. He was good at his job, and he could even be friendly. When he had nothing better to do.

25

Sadly, the good days didn't last long. The insurgents got cockier and started pushing us harder, week after week. We got used to waking up under fire. A loaded truck struck the green gate and exploded, wounding two soldiers. A man in a suicide vest blew up the check-point down the road, killing an interpreter and wounding a soldier.

We went outside the wire most days, and Butter, Viper, and I took turns in the lead. I was shocked to find that being in the back was harder than being in front. The tension didn't ease, but there was little I could do but hope that the lead K9 would find the IEDs and stay alive.

That Tuesday was Butter's turn to lead. We went to the village down the road to look for the explosives that insurgents used to make IEDs. Butter and Brown took us to the compound. We divided into three teams and searched every house.

Silver and I got the two in the middle and made short work of them. Searching in the mud houses in Kandahar is easy, you see. They're not like American houses, with their garages, basements, and attics full of furniture, appliances, and stuff. These houses are tiny, just a room or two, and mostly empty but for maybe a chest, a rug, and the curtains that serve as doors. A well-trained K9 will breeze through them in no time. It would be a piece of cake if it weren't for the people.

I don't think they like us.

People here are quiet and grim, and they smell like they're afraid of us. Even today. As I entered the house through the curtain, a woman in red kneeled on the ground, washing a half-naked kid. Another kid watched, exploring his nose. As soon as she saw me, the woman jumped back and the kids started screaming. They didn't try to pet me, let alone offer me a snack. I wouldn't take it since I'm on the job, but it would be nice! But that never happens. I wonder why.

We finished searching our part, and we joined the others. They hadn't found anything either. We filed behind Butter to return to the base. Silver and I were the tail that day, breathing everybody else's dust. I wish we were leading, I thought, when I heard the shots.

We dropped to the ground to take cover. That's when I heard Butter scream.

I leaped forward, but Silver pulled me back to the ground and kept me there.

"No! You can't help her, and you'll get yourself shot!"

She held me down as our soldiers returned fire, turning the world into a cloud of dust. Viper, Sabrina, and a few soldiers took off after the insurgents. I led the rest back inside the wire.

I wanted to stop to check on Butter, but Silver said no.

"The sooner we're back, the sooner we can take care of her. Her life depends on you leading us inside the wire."

I've never sniffed my way back faster. As soon as we got through the gate, I ran to Butter's stretcher and squeezed between the soldiers carrying her. Brown, her handler, was holding her paw.

"How are you doing, girlfriend?"

"I'm OK, Guinness. Thank you for bringing us back."

A weight lifted off my chest when I heard her speak, even though I knew she was lying. She was anything but OK, a shivering mass covered in blood. Brown, his black face gray, kneeled to tighten the tourniquet around her paw. Silver opened her K-9 first-aid kit to get a needle and tubing. Butter didn't even flinch when Silver started an IV.

I licked her nose and sat by her head.

"You'll be all right, Butter. You'll be like new in a day or two."

"Thanks, Guinness. I need to rest now."

She closed her eyes. Oh boy, how I was burning to jump on her and shake her awake. But Silver and Brown were better at helping her, so I stayed put.

She just lay there as they listened to her lungs and checked her belly. I wanted to help, but I didn't know what to do, so I just sat there until Viper came, panting and covered in dust.

"How's she doing?"

"Not great. They called for a helicopter. It should be here any moment."

He sat by my shoulder as we watched the helicopter land inside the wire. It lifted so much dust that we could barely see the soldiers loading Butter's stretcher. Brown climbed in too, and they took off, raising more dust.

That evening, as Viper and I lay in our crates, Butter's empty cage between us burned a hole in our souls.

"You think she'll make it?"

Viper sighed.

"I don't know. But she won't be back."

26

Life in Kandahar was not the same without Butter, As day after day went by without news from her, we walked around the base doing our jobs like a bunch of zombies. We were in mourning, even those who weren't close to Butter. We went on mission after mission to apprehend the insurgents but got nothing. One day we took four of them into custody, but none of them admitted to shooting Butter.

"Even if they didn't do it," Viper said, licking a scratch on his hind paw, "they know who did. I'd take care of it in an hour if they left them with me. They'd have no secrets after that, I promise you."

"I didn't know that was allowed. I've never participated in an interrogation. Have you?"

"Of course. I wasn't the one to ask the questions, but I was there. My handler said that my presence encouraged the subject to cooperate."

He licks his paw with a self-satisfied expression that makes me want to bite off his nose. But I remember that he's Butter's friend too, and I get over it.

"Did you bite them?"

"Not quite."

"What did you do, then?"

"I barked."

That sounds easy. I file that for later, in case I ever need to persuade somebody of something. Just bark at them. But I'm curious. Viper may be an ice-hole, but he's been places and has seen things. He knows a lot of things I don't.

"Did you ever bite a human?"

"Of course. Didn't you?"

"In training, of course. But I mean for real."

"A few times."

"Why?"

"They were bad people that I needed to apprehend. What did you want me to do? Ask them to stop?"

"Did they get hurt?"

"Of course. That's the whole idea. If you don't hurt the perps, they won't stop. Then you may have to do something more drastic."

"Like what?"

"Like kill them."

I stop to digest that. I did, once, kill a squirrel. Mom got upset. So did Jones. I promised I'd never do it again. I didn't really mean to kill him; I was just playing, but I shook him, and he died. That was bad enough. But killing a human?

"Did you kill any people?"

Viper's eyes are dark holes as he looks at me.

"I can't answer that, Guinness."

"So you did. How?"

"How what?"

"How do you kill a human?"

"Why do you want to know?"

Good question. I never considered killing anyone. But what if I found the guy who shot Butter?

"Just out of curiosity."

Viper doesn't believe me, but he answers anyhow.

"You bite deep and crush their throat. None of this nonsense with arms and legs. A good throat bite should do it."

I get a flashback to my first mission when I found the kidnapped little girl and the perpetrator, but I lost Shorty. I was desperate to go back for him, but there was no time. I had to go it alone. I did my best, but I almost lost that fight. Until I grabbed the perp's throat. That was the end of that fight, but I never realized that I could have killed him. That's scary.

"But…"

I don't get to finish since Silver comes to pet me. Her eyes are red and swollen, and I know she's got something awful to tell me.

"Guinness, I just spoke to Butter's handler."

"And?"

"The good news is that she's going to make it. The vest stopped the bullets from penetrating any of her internal organs."

I suddenly feel happier than I've ever been.

"But…"

"But?"

"But the bullets destroyed her leg. It was so bad that the surgeons couldn't save it. They had to amputate."

"To do what?"

"They had to cut off her leg. Butter will make it, but she can't come back."

27

I lay in my crate thinking about Butter: her luminous eyes; her silky golden ears; her warm, gentle tongue. I'll never see her again. Just like Mom, Jones, and Shorty, she disappeared from my life. I can't understand that. How can somebody you love just disappear? And, if even those you love just vanish from your life, who can you trust? How can you trust anyone? What if Silver vanishes next?

In the crate next to mine, Viper smells my distress.

"That's life, Guinness. People come, people go. There's nothing you can do."

"But then what's the point?"

"What's the point to what?"

"What's the point to life? If you can't trust anyone, ever, to always be there?"

He lays his nose on his paws and flattens his ears.

"I don't know, Guinness. I'm not smart enough. I just eat my breakfast, work through my training, and go on patrol trying to do my job and keep Sabrina and the others alive. Day after day after day. I don't want to think about the day when I'll step on a mine. Or even worse, miss it, and have Sabrina or one of the men step on it. If I did, I don't know that I could go on doing my job. And doing my job is all I know. My job is who I am. So, I'll leave those questions to those smarter than me, and I'll just do my job the best I can."

I choked. Surely there should be more to life than doing your job every day. There should be fun, and friendship, and laughter. And love.

I looked at Viper, The Fur Missile, all eighty pounds of him lean muscle and iron will, and for the first time ever, I felt sorry for him. For all his macho bravado, he was nothing but a lonely, loveless old dog. That made me so sad. What's the point of life without love? I'm miserable, but at least I got to love Mom and Jones and Shorty and Butter. And I still have Silver. Viper only has his job.

Life went on like it always does. Breakfast and training and patrol and sleep, then repeat, day after day. Viper and I took turns leading the patrol, and it was like Butter never happened.

"When will Brown return?" I asked Viper one day. "He may have news about Butter."

"It's gonna be a while," Viper said. "He's got to train a new dog first."

That took my breath away like a stab in my heart.

"What do you think happened to Butter?"

He shrugged without answering, and that made me sick to my stomach. He knows something he doesn't want to tell me. That can't be good news.

But the good news wasn't far. One morning Silver let me out of my crate and hugged me, her eyes full of light.

"Guinness, guess what?"

"What?"

"We're going home."

"Home?"

"Yes. Our deployment is over. In less than a month, we're going home. We'll eat popcorn and bacon and cookies. We'll go hiking without sniffing for bombs. We'll walk through the snow instead of dust, we'll eat real food instead of MREs, and we'll be on our own for a change. Don't you love that?"

"I sure do."

The news that we're out of here gave me hope. And an idea.

"Can we visit Butter?"

"I don't see why not. I don't know where she's at, but I'll find out."

I was on a high after that. Every morning I asked Silver whether the day had come. It hadn't, but it was close. Until one day she said:

"Tomorrow, Guinness. Today is our last patrol. We're going home tomorrow."

I jumped around like a puppy. Viper looked at me like I was nuts. But I couldn't wait to go on patrol that morning. That was my last one. An informer had told us about a cache of weapons in a nearby field, and Silver and I were leading the patrol.

We got out of the wire as usual: me first, Silver following thirty feet behind me on her leash, then the others filing behind her at a safe distance.

I sniff my way down the road to the village. I've done it so many times, it's a piece of cake. Everything smells OK. I get to the eight-foot wall surrounding the compound, and I take the narrow path between the mud wall and the scraggly bushes. I'm extra meticulous along that path, stepping gingerly and sniffing every bush. I'm about to turn the corner to the fields when I hear something behind me.

I turn around and look back.

Something flew over the wall and fell on the path, twenty feet behind me. It hit the ground and rolled toward Silver. I turn around to catch it.

"No! Guinness, run!" Silver screams, letting go of the leash. "Run!"

Run? Run where?

"Run," she screams again, then drops to the ground.

I freeze.

What the heck do I do? I don't understand her command. Run?

Even worse, I feel alone without her on the leash. But she said run. Run after what?

I look ahead, looking for whatever she sent me after. There's nothing.

I turn around to go back. I take one step, and something punches me in the chest and throws me to the ground. I land on my head in a cloud of dust. What the heck happened? I wake up all alone in a world of silent orange dust.

Then I smell the explosive, and I remember.

The grenade blowing up. Silver, telling me to run.

I run back.

She's there, all alone, covered in dust, lying face down on the ground just where she took cover. I call her, but she doesn't move. I lick her hand. It's salty, and it smells like blood.

28

I lay on her and lick her ear to wake her up, but she won't move.

"Hey, Silver! Wake up! We need to go!"

I grab onto her uniform to drag her back, but the men push me away. They turn her over. Her mouth is open, and her dark open eyes stare at the sky. I call her again.

"Silver! Let's go!"

I jump on her, but someone drags me away.

They lay her on a stretcher like they did with Butter. Good. We're going back inside the wire to take care of her. I go to the lead to bring them back to camp since that's my job, but they won't let me. Maybe because she's not on the leash to follow me and give the warning? I walk behind the stretcher as Viper takes us back to camp.

We enter the green gates. I wait for them to start an IV and put on a tourniquet, but they don't. What the heck? Did they forget?

I pull her first-aid kit from her vest and drop it on her to remind them what they have to do. I bark my heart out to urge them, but they just stare at me with teary eyes. One even tries to pet me. I bare my teeth and growl.

"Are you crazy, people? Do something! Help her! Call the helicopter! We're going home tomorrow! She needs to wake up."

She doesn't.

"I'm sorry, Guinness. She won't wake up."

I stare at Viper like he's lost his mind.

"She has to. We're leaving tomorrow."

He looks at me down his arrogant black nose, and if I didn't know any better, I'd think he's crying. But he isn't. Dogs don't cry, especially Viper, who doesn't love anyone or anything but his job.

I go back to Silver and shake her, but she doesn't wake up. They try to drag me away, but I won't let them touch me. I bare my teeth and growl until Sabrina, Viper's trainer, opens up her first-aid kit and takes out a syringe and a needle. I sigh with relief.

"Finally! I thought none of you was going to do anything. What took you so long?"

"Sorry, Guinness," she says, plunging the needle in my neck.

29

I wake up in a kennel. I don't often do kennels, but I know the smell: dog poop and pee, food, disinfectant. But this one's different. Besides all those, this one also smells like blood, fear, and death.

I look around: concrete floors, bare white walls, and kennels full of sick bandaged dogs wearing the cone of shame, so they can't clean up their wounds. Some sleep, some bark, some cry. Nobody looks at me.

I try to remember how I got here, but I can't. I went on a mission. The dust. The explosion. Silver, laying on the ground. The trip back, when they wouldn't let me lead. The men, staring at me instead of looking after Silver. Sabrina's needle.

The pain explodes in me like a grenade. Something chokes me, and I can't breathe. I pant, trying to get air through the tightness in my throat, but I can't. The room spins, then it turns dark. I lay down and close my eyes, waiting for it to go away. When I open them again, a dozen dogs stare at me.

"Where am I?"

"You're at the Holland Military Working Dog Hospital at Lackland Air Force Base, the best K-9 hospital in the country. What's wrong with you?"

I'll be darned if he doesn't look just like Butter. The same golden silky coat, the same ears. But he's not Butter. He has all his legs.

"I have no idea. How about you?"

"I got wounded in Iraq. I got some shrapnel in my hind leg, but they say I'll be better soon and I can go back. You?"

"I was on patrol in Afghanistan. We were looking for weapons."

"And?"

"And...my handler, Silver. She died."

"She stepped on a mine?"

That's a loaded question. If she did, that would technically be my fault since I failed to signal it. Or her fault if she missed my signal.

"No. Somebody threw a grenade."

"That sucks," a sable German shepherd says. He's all the way to the left, and his head is so bandaged he looks like a mummy. But he sniffs toward me, and I sniff back.

"Are you a German shepherd?" he asks.

"Yep."

"Me too. Name's Primus. You?"

"Guinness."

"Now that's a good name. You like beer?"

"I sure do."

He laughs, and chokes, and laughs again. He's old and arthritic, and he sounds like an old smoker, but he's one of my people.

"What happened to you, Primus?"

"It's a long story. But the bottom line is I got into a load of ammunition just as it blew up, and I lost my eyes."

The enormity of that strikes me. Losing your eyes! How can you live without them? The only thing worse than that would be losing your nose.

"I'm sorry, Primus."

"Yep. Not fun. But at least I still have my nose. What's up with you, girl? How are you hurt?"

"My handler died."

"That's too bad. But how are you hurt?"

I stop to think. I don't know the answer.

"I don't know yet."

"What hurts?"

"My soul?"

"Have you got PTSD?"

"What's that?"

"Post-Traumatic Stress Disorder. That's when the stress is too much, and we can no longer function."

"Of course not. That's got to be for sissies."

"That's what I thought until I saw my partner Ben," the Butter lookalike says. "It's real. I've never seen a braver dog. I don't even know how many lives he saved. Then one day, he just turned off. He was afraid of noises and growled at people. He could no longer do his job. That was hard to watch; I'd worshipped him since I was a pup. But he just lost his mojo."

"Why?" Primus asks.

He shrugs.

"I guess it got to be too much? The stress. The deaths. The losses. Either way, he couldn't go back to work."

"What did he do?"

"They tried to rehabilitate him, then they put him up for adoption. Dunno what happened next, but I sure hope they found him a family."

"How about his old trainers? I heard that retired dogs get to live with their old trainers and their families until they cross the rainbow bridge."

"Maybe he didn't have any? I don't know."

"Hey, Guinness?" Primus's old, whitened snout points to me as if he could see me, though I know he can't. He's got bandages all over his eyes.

"Yes, sir."

"We German shepherds need to stick together. Let me know if you need anything. I'll do my best to help you."

I stare at him. He's locked in his kennel, he can't see squat, and the curve of his spine tells me that his days of running and jumping are over. He's an old-timer, while I'm barely three years old, and he offers to take care of me. I'm ashamed.

"Thanks, Primus. I really appreciate it. Same here, you know. Let me know how I can help."

He nods toward me, and his shaky chin lands on his paws.

"I'd do anything for another set of eyes. Let me know if you'd like a companion."

30

The vet was slight and fast, with soft nimble fingers that smelled kind. She checked me from my muzzle to my tail, poking and prodding every inch of me. She X-rayed my hips and my chest and got enough blood out of me to build an extra dog. She took me to exercise and to training and tested me in every way.

I didn't do so good.

She didn't tell me, but I heard her speak to my lieutenant.

"I have bad news. Guinness won't be back."

"Why not?"

"She's got PTSD."

"I thought that only happened to people."

"Dogs are people too, you know."

She sounds irked. I like that, even though that's not how I'd put it. I'd say people are people, too, even if they aren't dogs.

"So what, then?"

"She'll have to go through rehab. We'll see how she does. If she does well, we may find her a civilian job. If not, I hope we can rehab her as a pet."

The lieutenant's hackles rise at the same time as mine.

"A pet? You've got to be kidding."

"Pets are people too. They make families happy, and they teach them the value of unconditional love."

The lieutenant bailed out. So did I.

Rehab was nice. They train you like you're a puppy, praising and rewarding you for every little thing. But the best was that Primus was there too, and we got to hang out.

I lent him my eyes, and he lent me his wisdom. We did everything together. And, since he could still smell, we could communicate without needing to see each other.

"They're a good pair," the vet said after watching us at rehab one day. "They help each other. Let's find them a home together."

The therapist shrugged.

"That would be nice, but it sounds unlikely. Who'd ever want two German shepherds, one blind, one with PTSD?"

"Let's spread the word and work on it."

That's how we found Tony. Or, more like, how Tony found us.

31

I knew something was up when the tech came to take me out of my kennel one evening. In the hospital, stuff only happens in the morning: feeding, walking, training, doctor's visits. The evenings are for laying around and telling stories unless there's an emergency.

When the tech opened my door, the whole kennel woke up and stuck their noses to watch him put on my leash.

"Who's sick?" Primus asked.

"Guinness," Goldie said, his eyes dark with worry.

Primus groaned.

"Hey Guinness, you OK?"

"Yep."

"Where you going?"

"Dunno."

"Call if you need help."

"Thanks."

The tech took me to an exam room. I wondered what this was all about since I didn't feel any worse than usual, but I didn't have much time to worry. The vet came in, followed by a stocky, dark-haired man.

He smelled of cigar smoke and booze, which I hadn't smelled in forever, but the strangest thing about him was that he was not in uniform.

"Hi, Guinness. This is Tony."

"Hi, kid. How ya doing?"

I look straight into his eyes. They're dark, unblinking, and warm.

"Fine, thanks," I say, slapping my tail to the floor. "You?"

"She's doing well. Guinness is healthy and very smart, but she went through some rough times."

"What happened to her?"

"I can't tell you that, but I can tell you that she got hurt while she was on a mission."

"She got shot, eh?"

"Sorry, Tony, her history is confidential."

"Where did she get shot?"

"Sorry, Tony. No can do. What do you think?"

"She's beautiful. Sleek, shiny, and almost black, but for those brown eyebrows. I bet you can't even see her in the dark. She's well trained, you said?"

"Best trained dog this side of the Atlantic."

Tony nodded and sat in the metal chair by the desk.

"Guinness, come."

I went and sat in front of him, as expected.

"Down."

I downed.

"Bark."

I barked.

The whole kennel erupted, barking up a storm. The walls shook with noise as they outdid each other.

"What's up?"

"You OK, girl?"

"You need us?"

I barked again.

"I'm good, thanks, guys. I'll call if I need you."

They went quiet.

"Wow. That was something else," Tony said.

"Yep. They all are buddies. Especially her old buddy Primus. He's blind. They go everywhere and do everything together. We'd like to find them a home together."

"I wasn't looking for two dogs. I only need one. Is that one trained too?"

"Of course. Primus is a K-9 vet. He lost his sight when he found a cache of explosives."

"German shepherd?"

"Yes."

Tony shrugs.

"I dunno. I wasn't planning on two dogs. That complicates things. Two dogs take a lot of room. Like how do you even fit them in the car?"

The vet crossed her arms, leaned against the wall, and said nothing. That's a negotiation tactic Shorty taught me when we went shopping for second-hand camping gear. "The one who speaks first takes the merchandise home," he said. He was right.

Tony sighs and stares at the vet.

"With two dogs, you need two of everything: Two dog beds. Two leashes. Twice the food."

He waits for her to say something. She doesn't.

"Can't you find another place for the other one? I'd be glad to chip in his adoption fee."

"Sorry, Tony. No can do. They're a team: She's his eyes; he's her strength. They're better together than they are apart. They come as a team."

"But I don't need a team. I just need a dog. A protection dog."

"I'm sure you can find one. Just google "protection dog." There are hundreds of them. European bloodlines, Schutzhund, champion parents, whatever."

"Yep. You buy them online, then it turns out you paid thousands of dollars for a dud."

"That's unfortunate, isn't it?

Tony glares at her, then turns to me.

"Hey, Guinness. Wanna come home with me? We'll live the good life—no dog food for you, girlfriend. You'll get spaghetti and meatballs, and lasagna every day. And bacon. You like bacon?"

I drool, trying to pretend it isn't me. But he sees it and thinks he's got me hooked.

"Hey, girl, I'll go all out for you. I'll even get you a cat to chase. What do you think?"

I can't help but laugh, and he sees it. His eyes shine brighter as he pats my head.

"Wanna come?"

I turn away.

"Not without Primus. Sorry."

The vet smiles.

"Tony, would you like to see Primus?"

Tony shrugs.

"What's there to see? A dog is a dog is a dog. Are you sure you won't let me have her?"

"Sure."

"Oh well. I guess I'll have to get a bigger car."

The tech goes back to bring Primus. He finds me by the smell, and I lick his nose to tell him that everything is OK. He sighs and sits by me, his shoulder touching mine, as usual.

Tony stares at us, and I'll be darned if I don't see tears in his eyes. But he turns away.

"I'll go get the car."

The vet hugs us.

"You'll be OK, guys. Tony's a little weird, but he's OK. He's my ex-sister-in-law's friend, and he vouched that he'll be good to you. Don't let him get away with anything, but do your best to keep him safe."

A horn blasts outside. We head out, walking shoulder to shoulder, and jump in the back of Tony's black SUV. The leather seats smell like tobacco, hamburgers, fries, and something that I can't define.

Tony looks at us, curled next to each other in the back seat.

"I guess they fit in," Tony says. He slams the door, turns on the engine, and we're on our way.

"Hey, Guinness, you smell this?" Primus whispers.

"Yes. What is it?"

"Cocaine, baby. Life is about to become interesting."

32

Primus was right. Our lives did become interesting.

Our new home was beautiful and big enough for twenty dogs, let alone some people. It stood alone, surrounded by acres and acres of birches, maples, and pines guarding a blue pool reflecting the sky. It was quiet and peaceful but for birds and squirrels since no one else lived there but for Tony, Primus, and me. People came to cook, clean, and tend the grounds, but they all left before dusk. In the evenings, it was just the three of us.

The vet was right. Tony grew on you. He was funny and kind when he wasn't an ice-hole, which happened often. And he talked to us like no other human ever did.

"You know, guys, I can talk to you since I know you won't go to the newspapers with any of it, but there's nobody else I can trust. My ex-wife, she can't wait to go and spill the beans. But we had a prenup, you know, so I told her:

"Evy, you're gonna be famous, or you're gonna be rich. Pick one. If you keep your mouth shut, like the prenup says, you'll be loaded. Sure, the media wants your story. What did he have for breakfast? How often did he shower? How was he in bed? They won't pay you much, but you think you'll go on TV, flash your mascara, and some big shot in Hollywood will be thunderstruck and make you the next movie star. I don't think so, baby, but it's your choice.

"She didn't go to the newspapers, but she started hating me even more. Even though she rolls in my money. She's not grateful, that one. Neither is my brother, Pig. You'll meet him soon, I bet. He can't stay away. He tries to be in my good graces, so he comes to visit and kisses my butt, but I bet he'd sell me for a burger if he could. He can't wait for someone to kill me, you know. That may happen, you know. In my line of business, few live to retire. And your family won't partake of the risks, but they feel entitled to what you earn, whether they're your wife, your kids, or your brother. Thank God I never had kids. I was always careful, you know? But I have Evy and Pig looking forward to my funeral. I'll be darned if I won't play one last trick on them. Just wait until Thursday."

On Thursday, Tony's lawyer came by. He was tall, unsmiling, and torn between holding on to his leather briefcase or to his combed-over white hair that looked about to fly away.

He let go of his hair just long enough to shake Tony's hand.

"Hi, Lance. Thanks for coming. I want you to redo my will."

"Your will? But you just changed it six months ago."

"I've changed my mind. There, meet my buddies, Guinness and Primus. I want you to write a will that leaves them everything I've got."

Lance turned purple and forgot his hair.

"But Tony, these are dogs."

"Observant, as usual. Thanks for pointing that out. That's why I pay you the big bucks."

"You're kidding, yes?"

"Not in the least. I want my dogs to be well cared for if something happens to me."

"Your brother and your ex-wife will get mad."

"That's the point, Lance. That's exactly why I'm doing this."

"But Tony, dogs don't need money. They don't buy houses or shoes or vacations. What would they need money for?"

"To stay alive and safe if something happens to me. I want Guinness and Primus to have a comfortable retirement. They're always here for me, and they do their best to keep me alive. There's no one else who doesn't want me dead. Not even you, Lance."

"Tony!"

"But we're about to fix that. You'll be my trustee, and you'll manage the funds for the dogs, should I croak. You'll pay for their upkeep and keep them comfortable, safe, and happy. Capisce?"

Lance stares from Primus to me, then back to Tony.

"Are you serious?"

"Totally. Draft the will, and I'll sign it next week."

Later that evening, when Tony was on the phone with a business associate discussing a new shipment, I asked Primus:

"What was that all about?"

"Tony loves us. Even more, he hates his family. He wants to see them squirm, so he makes sure they'll get nothing when he dies."

"But he's not old, Primus. And he's not walking into IEDs in Afghanistan either. Why would he die?"

"Land mines come in all sorts, Guinness. And Tony walks through them every day. That's why he got us. Kinda like insurance. His life is a nest of hate and worry."

"I can't imagine what I would do with money. Have you ever owned money?"

"Once. My handler gave me a dollar to take to the McDonald's drive-through to buy a burger."

"Was it good?"

"The best I ever had. I paid for a plain burger, but they gave me a bacon cheeseburger with all the trappings. It was phenomenal. Money is good, Guinness. It buys good things."

I like cheeseburgers, but I'd rather that Tony lives a long life. I'm getting really tired of death.

Primus looks at me with his blind eyes. He can't see me, but he can see straight into my soul.

"Death is part of life, kid. One of these days, I'll be gone. With the way Tony lives his life, he may be gone too. You can't anchor your life around someone else. It's between you and God."

"God?"

"He's up above, taking care of us all. He's always there when we need him, and he listens to our prayers."

Primus's empty eyes look up to the sky as if he's seeing God. I try to bite my tongue. I want to spare his feelings, even though he's clearly lost his mind, but I can't.

"If God is so good and powerful, how come he didn't save your eyes? How come he didn't spare Silver?"

"His ways are hard to understand. But he's all beauty and love."

I sigh and lay my nose on my paws. I hope God watches over Primus. And over Tony. I know he's not watching over me—I'm not worth it. But, if he takes care of those two, I'm all set.

33

God must have been busy that day.

It was just a day like all the others. We got up and had bacon and pancakes while Tony drank three espressos and smoked his cigar; then we loaded in his car and drove to take care of business.

We had a routine. Primus walked with Tony wherever he went while I waited in the car by the open window, ready to join them if they called me. Primus looked really sharp since Tony got him a pair of dark doggles that covered his eyes, so nobody knew he was blind. He stayed glued to Tony's knee: walked with him, sat with him, and growled whenever Tony raised his voice. And, of course, he kept his nose open to warn him if anything smelled fishy.

My job was to sit in the car, waiting to be called. It never happened, and I was bored to death. Why should I always stay in the car when they had all the fun? I threw a hissy fit, but Tony explained that Primus was his deterrent while I was his weapon.

"When they see Primus, they'll think twice before they try anything. It would be just the same with you. But if there's any trouble, you can join us in a flash, while Primus would have trouble finding his way between all the crap."

That made sense since there was a lot of crap. Tony's business took place in warehouses and garages rather than offices. He walked in there in his fancy suit, talked to some mechanic in soiled overalls, exchanged his bag for another, then came back to the car, and off we went. It wasn't a strenuous job.

It was no different that morning. I watched Tony and Primus go to the warehouse, then I sat by the window, watching the street. It was a drizzly wet fall day in the wrong part of town. The warehouse wasn't pretty. Nor was the street: heavy trucks shook the road, cars fouled the air with their fumes, and people with umbrellas bumped into each other as they jumped over puddles. But I had a blast. I always loved the rain, almost as much as I love snow, but since my time up close and personal with the dust in Kandahar, I can't get enough of it. I also love the mud. It squishes between your toes when you step in it, and it soothes your feet. Primus loves it too. I'll take him for a nice long walk when we get home, I think. At home, we come and go as we please since there's no one there for miles. Except for the squirrels, of course.

As I imagine chasing the squirrels, I see a man in a black hoodie enter the garage, and my hair stands on my neck. Why? I wonder. Then I realize. He smells like explosives.

I fly out the window just as the metal door closes behind him. I need to find another way in. I sprint around the building, looking for an opening, but there's nothing.

I find an open window up high in the back. I sprint to gather momentum, but it still takes me three tries to grab onto the frame with my front paws. I push myself up with the back end and land on the concrete floor just as the first shot rings.

I roll, jump on my feet, and start tracking. I follow my nose around parked trucks, dismantled cars, leaking batteries, and piles of tires. I run like I never ran before, when I hear one more shot, then a scream. It's Primus, and my heart freezes in my chest. This is not the call for help; it's a scream of pain.

I leap over a pile of tires to see dust rising behind a metal container. The next shot rings as I jump on top of it. I find myself above the hoodie man with the gun.

Six feet away, Tony lays unmoving on the concrete floor, his fancy suit dripping red. Primus, his breath a spray of blood, holds a tight grip on the man's leg as the man points his gun to his head.

I leap at the man's throat, but I miss. I grab onto his arm and drag him to the ground. His head slams the ground with a hollow sound, just as I hear another shot. A sharp pain stabs my side and takes my breath away. I feel like I'm choking, but I don't let go until the man stops moving.

I finally take a breath, and it's like a grenade blew up in my chest. But I don't have time for it. I grab the gun and drop it a few feet away, then I check on Tony. His dark eyes are wide open, even the third one, a black hole in the middle of his forehead.

I move on to Primus, who lays panting on his side. His short, ragged breaths come out in red bubbles.

"Guinness?"

"Yes, partner."

"Thanks."

"What for?"

"For taking me with you. I know Tony didn't want me. He got used to me, but he didn't want me. If it weren't for you, I'd still be in that freaking kennel, eating kibble instead of dying on a mission."

"You aren't dead yet," I say, my voice breaking.

"I'll soon be. But thanks to you, I got to have the best time of my life, running free through the forest with my partner by my side, eating lasagna for dinner, and dying like a soldier should. Thanks, Guinness."

I choke, and I don't know if it's because of his words or the wound in my chest.

"Hang in there, Primus. Help's coming. I can hear the sirens."

"Not for me, baby, I'm done. But come here. I want to smell you one more time."

I lick his nose. It's cold and wet, and it tastes like blood. I rearrange his doggles, so he looks sharp as the sirens choke and the door slams open.

"Drop your weapons! Nike, search."

A K-9 in a bulletproof vest explodes through the door, followed by his handler. He sees Primus, then me, and stops dead in his tracks.

"What the heck? Who are you?"

" Sergeant Primus, Marine K-9, retired. This is Corporal Guinness, MPC K-9. You?"

"Corporal Nike K-9."

"Corporal Guinness disarmed your perpetrator. The gun's under the desk. But she needs medical help. Get your handler."

"Yes, sergeant."

By the time we get to the hospital, Primus is no longer with us. All that's left lying next to me is his thick, sable fur and his doggles. Everything that made Primus be Primus— his generous soul, his dauntless courage, his loyalty, and his wisdom - left to join Tony.

I hope they're together up above. God would better appreciate what a fantastic K-9 he got, because I can't believe that that beautiful, heroic canine soul vanished into nothing. The world deserves better than that.

34

This hospital is nothing like the K-9 hospital I was at before; it's small, dark, and weird. And it doesn't have my buddy, Primus.

The dogs here don't look like K-9s. They even have a few cats, for God's sake, and I'll be darned if I don't smell a ferret some-where! But that breaks up the boredom. This is the first time I've gotten up close and personal with a cat, besides Jones's Whiskey. What evil creatures! They wait until you're half asleep, then start taunting you. There's a big orange one with a bandaged ear who's got a thing about Charlie, the small poodle mix across from her. She doesn't miss a chance to taunt him. I don't even know Charlie, but it's hard to watch.

She licks her paws with a pink tongue so raspy I can hear it from my cage.

"Hey, you rotten mutt. You think your human will come back to get you? A disgusting thing like you? Think again."

Charlie shivers, his weepy eyes scared.

"Who'd ever want a mangy mutt like you, huh?"

Charlie melts into the floor and looks away, pretending he can't hear her. He's not pretty, Charlie, nor terribly brave. But that's not a reason to be mean to him—just the opposite. One should be kind to those less lucky. That's what decency is.

"You stink. And you..."

I can't take it anymore. I bark like the mailman is coming, and the whole place goes quiet.

"Enough. Stop that right now, you useless evil feline, or I'll show you a thing or two. You hear me, Van Gogh?"

The orange fluffs up like a toilet brush and stares at me with his round yellow eyes. He hisses:

"How do you know my name, you K-9?"

"I'm with the CIA. I know everything. And I'm about to tell everybody what you did unless you stop that right now."

He hisses again, just to save face, then turns away and sticks his nose under his tail, pretending to fall asleep.

Ever since that, Charlie looks at me like I hung the moon, which is both funny and endearing. He asks me about the war, and I tell him stories. I tell him about Butter, how everyone loved her and what a heroic K-9 she was, even though she was a mutt. That gives him confidence. It also helps pass the time since I feel like I've been here forever. Being anywhere forever is not my thing, but it's not like I have a choice.

One day I get visitors. One's Lance, Tony's lawyer. The other one looks like a pig.

"There she is," Lance says, petting his white hair as usual.

Pig man looks at me with his porcine eyes buried in pink fat. He studies me from my nose to my toes.

"This?"

"Yes."

His fat lips tighten.

"You think she's going to make it?"

"That's what the vet said. She'll start rehab tomorrow. If everything goes well, she could go home in a few days."

"Home where?"

"That's why I brought you here. As Tony's executor, I have to arrange for Guinness's welfare. She's got money, you know. Whoever takes her in will be well rewarded. Since she's your brother's dog, I thought I'd ask you first."

Pig spits to the side.

"Did he really leave her everything?"

"Yep."

"He was out of his mind. I'll contest the will."

"Up to you. But remember, I made the will, and I made it well. Getting it invalidated is less likely than getting Tony to come back and change it. But suit yourself."

Pig glares at me and then turns to Lance.

"How about we make a deal? You agree that he was cuckoo, we get the will invalidated, and I give you 10 percent of everything."

Lance turns red.

"There's something called professionalism, you know. I'm a lawyer. I'm here to represent my client's wishes. They'd take my union card if I did what you suggest."

"How about 20 percent?"

Lance's hair stands up.

"I don't think you're listening."

"Hold your high horses, Mr. Professional. Where was your professionalism when you agreed to be Tony's lawyer? You knew darn well what kind of business he was in!"

"That was his business. Everyone, even killers, has a right to legal representation. I did nothing illegal for your brother. I only helped him with his legal issues."

"So you say."

"Listen, man, I don't care what you think. You want the dog or not."

"No."

"OK. Thanks."

"What will you do?"

"I'll talk to Evy. She may want the dog and the money that comes with her."

"You've got to be kidding. That shrew?"

"Well, besides you, she's the closest thing Tony had to a relative. I think she may want the dog, not as much for the money but for emotional reasons."

Pig stares at Lance like he grew a second head, then bursts into thick, dirty laughter that makes my skin crawl.

"Emotional reasons? Evy?"

Lance shrugs.

"You never know. Either way, it's none of your business since you don't want the dog. Let's go."

Pig looks at me again but doesn't move.

"How much will you pay to whoever takes her?"

"I don't know yet. I'll have to evaluate Tony's estate, withdraw the taxes and expenses, and see what's left. But it will be a generous allowance. She, and whoever takes care of her, should be comfortable."

Pig shrugs.

"He's not that ugly, after all. Is he house trained?"

"It's a she. Her name's Guinness. And she's a retired K-9 officer and a highly trained protection dog."

"Well, I think I'll take it after all. My poor brother would certainly prefer that she, and the money, stay in the family. I always looked out for his interests. I'll take her. When do I get my first check?"

"I'll hand you the first check when she leaves the hospital, then another every month after that. But I'll come to check on her. She should be well cared for."

"Of course. What are you saying? I know how to care for a dog."

"Good. I'll let you know when they discharge her, so you can be ready."

"I'm ready already. Hey, Lance, what happens to the money if she dies?"

"I don't know. Unless Guinness makes a will, which is unlikely, a judge will decide what happens to her trust."

"But logically, the money should go to whoever takes care of her, no?"

"I don't know that logic has much to do with it. Logic and law don't always line up. But don't worry about that. The vet assured me that she's doing well, and she will live."

"What about if she gets sick? Gets hit by a car? Or eats rat poison?"

Lance's eyes narrow as he studies Pig.

"Listen, mister. If I were you, I'd make sure nothing bad happens to Guinness. Once she's gone, so are the monthly payments. She's worth more to you alive."

"Of course, of course. I just wondered."

35

Life with Pig wasn't bad. Not good either. Life with Pig wasn't much of a life. He lived alone in a double-wide, and nobody ever came to visit. He took me for a walk in the morning, fed me, then left me alone until the evening walk.

I sat alone in my bedroom all day, day after day, listening to my thoughts and thinking about those I loved. I missed them all: Mom, Jones, Shorty, Butter, Silver, and Primus. Even Tony. I spent my time having imaginary conversations with them until I stopped caring about real things and real people.

When Lance came to see me, I laid in my room, and I wouldn't get up. He frowned.

"What's wrong with her?"

Pig shrugged.

"Nothing. That's what she does."

"Lay alone in the dark every day?"

"She's a dog. What do you want her to do? Play chess?"

Lance's face darkened.

"Listen, man. This is not what we agreed upon. You're supposed to take care of her and keep her happy."

"Sure. And you're supposed to pay me well."

"I did. You get a thousand dollars a month. The dog doesn't eat a tenth of that."

"I expected more."

"Too bad. It's not my fault that Tony's house was heavily mortgaged, the car was leased, and he didn't have much else. He liked to live well, and he blew his money."

"And how is that my fault?"

"That's not your fault, but you promised to care of Guinness."

"I do. I feed her, walk her, and keep her safe. What else do you want me to do, for God's sake? Marry her?"

Lance shook his head.

"This won't work. I'll find somebody else to take her."

"The sooner, the better."

It was déjà vu all over again. One family after another came and left. I don't know if it was me or whatever Pig told them, but nobody wanted me.

I was relieved. I was tired of loving people just to have them die. If Pig died tomorrow, I wouldn't give a damn. It was easier to not care.

People stopped coming.

I lay in my room, day after day, night after night, thinking about my people. I stopped eating. I no longer wanted to walk.

"This is no good," Lance said. "She looks worse every time I see her."

"Why don't you take her, then? The way she looks, I'll have to put her down before too long."

That gave me hope. If they put me down, maybe I can join Primus, Shorty, and Silver?

Lance shook his head.

"I'll see what I can do. But in the meantime, don't forget: no dog, no money."

Life went on, day after day of nothing but my memories. I was getting so feeble I dreamt awake. It was harder and harder to tell my dreams from reality, and I loved it. I was back with my people.

"How are you doing, Guinness?" Butter asked.

"I'm good. I'll come to join you soon."

"Join me? But I'm not dead."

"Not dead?"

"No. I just lost a leg, remember?"

"You did? Then who died?"

"Silver."

"Silver? Was he the Malinois?"

"That's Viper. Silver was your handler. Bridge Silver. Small, brown, and kind."

I wake up and try to remember Silver's face, but I can't. My brain is so fogged I don't recall much beyond the smells. The one that I remember best is Primus. He was my buddy, and he died.

They slowly come back to me: Primus, Silver, Tony, and Shorty. The pain is so excruciating that I wish I could die. If only I had another chance to find an IED, I wouldn't signal. I'd just step on it.

That fire would surely burn away this pain.

36

But Kandahar is almost as far as the moon, and there are no IEDs here. There's nothing and nobody but Pig stopping by once a day to bring water and kibble. Day after day, he's less real to me than my friends. Because, wherever they are, they love me. Pig doesn't.

I spend all my time in my corner, but I'm not really here. I'm somewhere far away, clamming with Shorty, chatting with Butter, chasing squirrels with Primus, or singing with Mom under the red trees in Jones's yard. I finally understand what that song meant. And I think it's my time to die.

I lay my nose on my paws, and I close my eyes.

"Hey, girlfriend, how are you doing?"

"Silver?"

"Who else? I'm glad to see you. How are you?"

"I miss you. I miss you terribly. But I'm coming soon."

"Coming where?"

"Coming to join you."

"What are you talking about?"

"They're talking about putting me down. I can't wait for us to get together, watch movies and eat popcorn. Do they have popcorn there? How about bacon?"

Silver shakes her head.

"No, Guinness. We don't eat here. We left our bodies behind, remember? We're only as real as moving shadows."

"But..."

A dark Malinois sits next to her.

"This is Bear. I finally found him."

Bear slaps his tail to greet me, just like Viper, and all of a sudden, I feel sorry for hating him all this time.

"Hi, Guinness. Silver told me about you. Thanks for looking after her for me."

"For you?"

Anger fills me, and I'm about to blow up, but I'm too weak.

Then the door opens, and I realize it was just a dream. There's nobody here but me.

"Guinness?"

A woman stands in the door, waiting for her eyes to adjust. She's a mess: crumpled scrubs, a brown ponytail, tired eyes needing sleep. Then she steps in the light, and for a moment, she looks like she's on fire.

My heart skips a beat. It's Silver! She came to get me.

"Hi, Guinness. I'm Emma."

She's not Silver.

She doesn't look like Silver, and she doesn't smell like Silver, either. She smells like sadness and loneliness. And she needs a shower. But she also smells like magic.

She sits near the door.

"How're you doing?"

Her voice is low and tired. She's not a talker, but she tries.

"You don't feel like chatting, do you? Neither do I. Life sucks."

"Yep."

"I came to meet you. I know you need a friend. So do I. I thought maybe we could get along."

I remember all those I've lost. Mom. Jones. Shorty. Butter. Silver. Primus. I can't do it again.

"I don't think so."

"Are you sure?"

I look away.

"I see. I'm sorry. Well, then. I have a long drive home, and I need to find a toilet and some coffee first. I'd better get going."

"Yep."

She sighs.

"Life stinks. My daughter hates my guts. My ex-husband got bored with his pretty wife. And I think someone's killing my patients."

Her phone beeps.

"That's Taylor, my daughter. Did you ever have puppies, Guinness?"

"Are you kidding? I've done nothing but train and sniff for IEDs ever since I was a pup."

"You didn't miss much, trust me."

I blink.

"You're right. Why should you trust me? I'm just a stranger."

She crosses her legs like she has to pee.

"I have to go, Guinness. I'm sorry it didn't work out."

She picks up her bag.

"I forgot. I brought you something. You like Italian? This is Bolognese, loaded with basil and garlic. Garlic kills worms, you know. I'm not saying you have them; I'm just telling you what it's good for."

She sets the container near my water bowl. The aroma of garlic hits me like a bullet, bringing me back to the evenings when Tony taught us to cook pasta.

"Good luck, old girl. I'll root for you."

Nobody called me old before, but that hits the spot. I feel like I've lived a few lives. I feel old enough to die.

She'd like to pet me, but she knows I don't want to be touched.

"Bye, Guinness."

She heads to the door with her open bag, messy hair, and crumpled pants. The scent of her loneliness makes me choke. She needs someone to look after her.

Not me.

She leaves.

I sigh, and the garlic fills my nose and makes me drool. There's also basil, pepper, Parmigiano Reggiano, beef, San Marzano tomatoes. And oregano.

I check it out. It's barely defrosted, and it lacks the pasta. It needs spaghetti—not farfalle, linguini, or rotini. The only correct pasta for this Bolognese is spaghetti, cooked al dente. Eight minutes in a large pot of very salty water, then drained and coated in the sauce. Serve with aged Parmigiano grated at the table. None of that cheap stuff you buy already grated. That's real Italian cooking. None better on Earth.

Tony loved giving us cooking lessons. He wiped his forehead with a kitchen towel as he stirred the sauce and checked the pasta. Primus and I watched, sitting in pools of drool.

"The pasta has to have a little bite to it and resist chewing, you know. Overcook it, and it's dead—nothing but mush. Don't forget the crushed red peppers; that's where the magic is. The heat sets your tongue on fire and wakes it up to the flavor."

I sniff it again. I'll just taste it, I think, then I discover that I inhaled it. It's not as good as Tony's, but it ain't bad. It's the first decent meal I've had in months.

As I'm licking it clean, I hear a car start in the driveway. She's leaving.

Good. I don't need this woman. I have my people. It can't be long now.

My stomach growls.

I set my nose on my paws and close my eyes.

She's a stranger. Why should I care about her? I'll soon join my people.

But Shorty has his father; Primus has Tony; Silver has Bear.

Tomorrow, Pig will bring me water and kibble. Lance may stop by to check on me. I'll just lay here, daydreaming of my friends. The same the day after tomorrow and the day after that.

Unless I go with the shaman. She needs a shower, but she's got magic. And she can cook.

What would life with her be like? I don't know, but it can't be much worse than rotting in the dark.

I remember Shorty: "Someday, you'll save somebody's life." But I didn't. Not his, not Primus's, not even Silver's. I haven't yet fulfilled my mission.

I struggle to stand, but I'm so shaky I have to sit down again. It takes me forever to get to the door, then to drag myself down the hallway. Shaman's got to be gone by now; she was desperate to pee.

But no. She's still here, setting up her navigator.

I stare at her through the driver's window. She glances back and stares straight into my eyes. She lights up like a Christmas tree.

"Really?"

I wag my tail.

"Of course."

She opens the back door. I push aside a Red Cross bag to make some room, then curl up and thump my tail.

"What are we waiting for?"

AFTERWORD

Thanks for buying my book. I hope you enjoyed it as much as I loved writing it. Please take a minute to leave a review. That may make the difference between this book being a bestseller or a flop. Thank you for giving me your precious time.

To read Mom's story, checkout www.RadaJones.com/Free-Story-2 . It's short, sweet and free.

BIONIC BUTTER, Book #2 in the K-9 Heroes series, is on preorder now.

If you'd like to know what happened with Guinness, check out MERCY in my ER Crimes series. But be advised that MERCY is a medical thriller, not a family-friendly dog memoir.

Visit RadaJones.com for more content, to sign up for updates, and to drop me a note. I love hearing from you!

Rada

ABOUT THE AUTHOR

Rada Jones was born in Transylvania, only ten miles from Dracula's Castle. Growing up between communists and vampires taught her that while humans may be fickle, one can always depend on dogs and books. That's why she read every book she could get, including the phone book – too many characters, too little action – and took home every stray she found, from dogs to frogs.

After immigrating to the US to join her husband, she pursued a medical education and then worked in the ER for years. However, she still speaks like Dracula's cousin.

When night shifts became too much, she left the ER to write. Her ER Crimes series feature serial killers, some nicer than others, and Dr. Emma Steele, an ER doc with a dark sense of humor, a moody daughter, and a love for wine. If blood and gore turn you on, check out OVERDOSE, MERCY, and POISON. If you're into dark humor, check out her medical essays in STAY AWAY FROM MY ER.

But if you're into dogs, the K-9 series is right for you. It started when Rada's beloved German shepherd, Gypsy, crossed the rainbow bridge. To bring her back, Rada wrote her in MERCY. Emma adopted Guinness, a quirky bacon-loving K-9, who took over her life.

Then Guinness insisted on telling her own story. When her friends followed, the K-9 HEROES series was born. BIONIC BUTTER is on preorder. Viper's story is on its way.

To sign for updates, check out RadaJones.com. To get in touch, email her at RadaJonesMD@gmail.com.

EXCERPT FROM MERCY

AN ER THRILLER

Chapter 46

Taylor woke up early that morning. Something felt odd. *Somebody's watching me.* She looked around. Nothing. Just her old bedroom, with the grass lamp, the starfish comforter, and the orange rocker in the corner. She rolled on her other side and went back to sleep.

Somebody's watching me.

She was in her room, alone. She was losing it. She sat up and rubbed her eyes, looking for her Crocs with her feet.

Something touched her. She jumped. A dog. A big dark dog. Staring at her.

Really?

Yep. Really. He lay there at the foot of the bed, staring at her. She stared back.

The dog didn't blink. This was a serious dog. A police dog? How did it get in the house? What was it doing there?

Mother said she was getting a dog. She did.

She'd been gone the whole day. She had a shift today—she kept a copy of her godforsaken schedule on the fridge. Somehow, in between, she had acquired this animal. Then she'd gone to work and left this dog for Taylor to deal with.

Taylor loved Thelma and Louise. She'd grown up with them. They were cute and cuddly, even though they yapped a lot. But this dog was different. It acted like a person.

Oh well. It's Mother's problem.

Taylor found her Crocs and went to get something to eat. Now that her morning sickness was over, she was always starved. Thankfully, she was slim and burned calories like crazy. Still, she felt like a hippopotamus. She was getting slower and thicker, but she was still always hungry.

She opened the fridge. Mustard, ketchup, mayo, milk. *Like really? Not even eggs? How's a growing woman supposed to handle this?*

She found a box of Cheerios. That would have to do. Lunch looked like a losing proposition unless she got her ass out to do some shopping.

Where's the new you? The new you who'll get a job, grow up, and become responsible?

Taylor flipped the bird to that thought, and grabbed the Cheerios and a box of Oreos. She poured Cheerios, lots of sugar, and milk in a bowl and grabbed a spoon. She dropped on the sofa and turned on the TV.

The dog sat in front of her, staring. His head obstructed the screen.

"What?" Taylor said.

The dog gurgled. It wasn't a bark and it wasn't a growl.

"What do you want?"

The dog gurgled again, staring at her bowl.

He's hungry. We have no dog food. We have no food, period. Thanks, Mom!

"We have no dog food," she informed him. She took a spoon of Cheerios.

The dog gurgled again. Staring her in the face, the dog clearly demanded to eat.

"Don't you get it? We have no..." The dog looked at her bowl like Taylor would look at a fudge Sunday.

He wants my Cheerios. Dogs don't eat people food!

She lifted the spoon to her mouth. The dog drooled, watching its progression like it was the Olympics. Taylor opened her mouth. She closed it.

"Fine. Be that way. They got soggy anyhow!" She put the bowl on the floor next to the sofa. "You happy now?"

The dog stared at her.

"What?"

The dog stared.

"What are you staring at me for? Eat it!"

The dog gave a short happy bark and cleaned the bowl in a blink. He sat in front of it and gave a quick bark. He looked at Taylor and wagged his tail. Once.

"Thanks." He went to lie down by the door.

Taylor scratched her head.

She got herself another bowl of cereal and watched for the dog to come back. He didn't.

She finished her cereal and went to clean up. Brushed her teeth, took a shower, got dressed.

The dog waited by the door.

He needs to go out.

There was no leash—they hadn't had a dog in years. Taylor found a soft belt. She walked slowly toward the dog. She wasn't sure he cared to be touched.

"Want to go out?"

The dog wagged his tail.

She slipped the loop of the belt over his head. She tightened it. He didn't seem to mind. She opened the door. The dog waited. For what?

"Let's go," Taylor said. The dog leapt out. He smelled the bushes, the stones, and the grass. He squatted at the gate.

"You're a girl!"

The dog looked at her and smiled. They took a long walk. Taylor hadn't done that ever since she'd tried to kill herself. She was surprised to see it was still spring. It felt like ages ago.

Back home, Taylor removed the belt. The dog looked at her. She scratched her behind the ears. The dog smiled again.

Back in the bedroom, her phone rang. She had forgotten her phone. Unbelievable. She never forgot her phone. Five missed calls. One was Mother, one was Father, three were Eric.

"Call me."

BUY MERCY
ASIN : B07VYVPFFF

EXCERPT FROM BIONIC BUTTER
A THREE-PAWED K-9 HERO

Chapter 1

The lamb aroma hits my nose with a vengeance. I open my eyes to Brown fixing my breakfast. He stirs some magic bits into the kibble, douses it with hot water, and the scent makes me drool.

"Lamb!"

I love lamb! It's my favorite, right there with beef, chicken, and fish. Especially the way Diane, my mom, cooks it. She stuffs it with garlic, then rubs it with a concoction of Dijon, rosemary, and thyme and cooks it on high heat so it stays pink inside. But Diane is at home, half a world away, and we're in Afghanistan, at our base in Kandahar. And this isn't lamb; it's the MRE, Meals Ready to Eat, version of it, and it stinks. But it still beats plain kibble.

"The heck lamb, that's ancient mutton," Viper growls, his voice thick with sleep. "It must have died of old age. I bet you they can smell it all the way in Helmand."

Viper's not a foodie. He'll turn up his nose at kibble, but give him a ball, and he'll work all day. That's why I get to finish his meals, and I'm grateful enough to put up with his obnoxious Belgian Malinois attitude.

"Helmand? You've got to be kidding. They've got to smell it from back home."

Guinness crawls out of her crate to practice her morning yoga. She lifts her snout in the air in an upward dog, then rears her rear in a downward dog, then shakes like she's been through mud, and she's good for the day.

No wonder. Not only is she slim, black and shiny, but she's young. Guinness is just three, while I'm six and a bit on the chubby side. But that's only because I'm a yellow Lab. I bet I'd look thinner in black.

As for Viper, he's as old as the hills. He was here before me, and he'll still be here when I'm gone. Unlike the rest of us, Viper lives for his job. Detecting explosives is all he wants to do. He's glad to be here, while everybody else, K-9s and humans, can't wait to go home.

"You guys are too picky. You'd complain if they fed you McDonald's fries with ketchup." I turn back to my food. The scent is potent; the taste not so much. It could use some salt, some cracked black pepper, and a better chef than Brown.

Guinness sighs.

"I could go for some fries, especially if they came with a cheeseburger." She picks up a bit of kibble here and there, sniffs it like she's looking for IEDs, then drops it to the side.

"Fries are nothing but salt and fat. You guys need to make better choices if you want to keep in shape." Viper says, turning away from his food.

Viper's an athlete. He gets his highs from working out. He's a health nut, the kind of K-9 whose reward is the ball instead of food. That's why he's nothing but lean muscle and iron will.

"You guys heard the plan for the day?" Guinness asks.

"More of the same, I bet. We take our handlers for their walk, then train them to look for explosives inside the wire, then dinner. Boring," Viper says.

"You don't think we'll go outside the wire?"

"I wish we were, but we've been out every day this week. Our humans need a day to recover."

"I do too," I say, licking my bowl clean. "I need my beauty sleep."

"You sure do." Viper snickers then leaps aside when I pretend to jump at his throat.

"No rest today, boys and girls," Guinness says, as Silver, her handler, slips her bulletproof vest over her head and buckles it.

"Like really? What's wrong with these people? Can't they ever take a day off?" I growl, eyeing Viper's bowl.

"The insurgents have different priorities." Viper nuzzles the bowl towards me just as Brown comes over with my bulletproof vest.

"It's our turn in the lead today, Butter. Are you ready?"

"Almost."

I grab a few mouthfuls from Viper's food as Brown buckles my bulletproof vest. I'm glad we're in the lead. In the back, you breathe everyone else's dust and you have no choice but to follow. In the lead, you get the cleanest air and set the pace. There's always a chance you'll step on a mine and blow up, of course, but I'm not worried. I'm no longer a rookie; this is my fourth deployment, and I learned to take my time. Better slow than dead.

"Your turn again?" Viper mumbles, as Sabrina, his handler, fixes him up like the rest of us. He's in the middle today, and he hates it. He'd rather lead, like we all do. Not today, Malligator.

The lieutenant briefs us.

"Today's mission is searching the village compound for explosive materials. The insurgents stepped up their game lately; we find new IEDs every day. They must have explosives hidden somewhere. We need to find and destroy them. Brown and Butter, you're the lead. Good luck."

The tall green gate topped with sharp spikes creaks open, and I step outside the wire. Brown follows me on his leash, thirty feet behind, while the others stay back at a safe distance. Guinness and Silver come last.

I stop to take in the terrain. Tan dust covers the scorched earth as far as the eye can see. Nothing moves other than the plume of smoke rising over the village, bruising the pale-blue sky. A few tortured bushes bake under the merciless sun. It's so hot that I feel grateful for the dust protecting my paws from the burn, as much as I hate breathing it.

Far behind, Viper barks.

"Don't rush, Butter. We have nothing better to do than to watch the dust all day."

"Shut up, Viper. She knows what she's doing better than you do."

That's Guinness, of course. But Viper's right. There's only that long we can stand this heat, we in our fur and our soldiers under heavy armor and equipment. I step forward, struggling to ignore the dust filling my nose as I sniff my way, looking for IEDs. But the dust is so light it's everywhere. There's no fighting it, no avoiding it, no ignoring it. The one thing you can do is accept it, and focus on the one thing that really matters: keeping us all alive.

BUY BIONIC BUTTER
ASIN : B08XKBGXN3

Printed in the USA
CPSIA information can be obtained
at www.ICGtesting.com
LVHW021552051123
763105LV00016B/1101